MASTERPIECE

BOOK TEN-THE WALKER FAMILY SERIES

BERNADETTE MARIE

5 PRINCE PUBLISHING

Digital ISBN: 978-1-63112-244-6

Print ISBN: 978-1-63112-245-3

Cover Art: Bernadette Soehner

Published by 5 Prince Publishing, PO Box 865, Arvada, CO 80001

ALSO BY BERNADETTE MARIE

THE MATCHMAKER SERIES

Matchmakers

Encore

Finding Hope

THE THREE MRS. MONROES TRILOGY

Amelia

Penelope

Vivian

THE ASPEN CREEK SERIES

First Kiss

Unexpected Admirer

On Thin Ice

Indomitable Spirit

THE DENVER BRIDE SERIES

Cart Before the Horse

Never Saw it Coming

Candy Kisses

ROMANTIC SUSPENSE

Chasing Shadows

PARANORMAL ROMANCES

The Tea Shop

The Last Goodbye

HOLIDAY FAVORITES

Corporate Christmas

Tropical Christmas

THE DEVEREAUX FAMILY SERIES

Kennedy Devereaux

Chase Devereaux

Max Devereaux

Paige Devereaux

For Stan,
Our life
Our Masterpiece

ACKNOWLEDGMENTS

For my FIVE masterpieces: *You are my everything! I love you all!*
For Mama, Sissy, and Daddy: *You were always my support team when I started something new, and you've always been. I love you.*
For Cate: *Thank you for polishing my masterpieces*
For Brenden: *It's been fun to watch you create all your masterpieces, and for me to take some of your knowledge and add it to Jessie's story.*
For my Book Hive: *Thank you for taking part in the journey of my creations.*
For my Readers: *Thank you for encouraging me to continue creating new masterpieces.*
For my Tribe: *Thank you for having my back.*

MASTERPIECE

A small heater under the desk kept Todd's feet warm as he went over the schedule for the upcoming week. He'd been thrown into the position of managing Lydia Morgan's reception hall business, and he was doing a fair job, but he missed his mornings on the Walker Ranch, watching the sunrise over the acreage.

Lydia would be back soon enough, he kept repeating to himself as he answered emails, ordered provisions, and readied himself for the next bridal party that would come through the door to book their event.

In the past three months, he'd stopped stumbling over himself trying to give them every detail. He'd quickly learned that they usually knew everything about the hall, since Lydia's website was top-notch. It was just customary to walk around and check it out.

His sister Bethany, who was taking over some other duties while Lydia was away, would do her best to meet him and help with the walkthrough, but she had her own life with her family and a career writing books alongside her husband, who wrote the best sci-fi Todd had ever read. So, he took on most of the duties, and if he had time to make it out to the Walker Ranch, he'd step in and do what he knew best, and that was working a cattle ranch.

But family, even family comprised mostly of dear friends, was important. Lydia was taking the needed time to heal, emotionally and physically. She'd been the random victim of a serial killer nearly a year ago, but she'd been the one to get away. Lydia had taken full advantage of the opportunities given to her to recover both physically and mentally. He was proud of her for doing so, because he couldn't even imagine what she went through.

The alarm chimed on his cellphone. He silenced it with a swipe of his finger and picked up the file for the next bride to walk through the door. And like clockwork, he heard the door open to the hall.

Todd stepped out from behind the desk and walked out to the hall which he'd set up with the lighting the bride had said she was looking for. He smiled when he heard the oooohs and ahhhs.

"Carlie Hanson?" He approached the party of six women who were taking in the room.

"I'm Carlie," the short blonde in the pack's front said as she held out her hand to shake his.

"Todd Walker. I'll be showing you around the venue today." His eyes lifted to the women that gathered with the bride and settled on the tallest of them, who must have been the bride's sister.

Carlie turned around to face the women. "This is my mother, Carol. My best friends Emily and April. And my maid-of-honor, my sister Jessie."

Jessie, he thought as he shook her hand and drank in the sight of her.

The other women were closer to Lydia's five-foot mark, but not Jessie. She nearly looked Todd in the eye and must have been six-foot tall.

"It's nice to meet you," he said as Jessie shook his hand.

"You too," she affirmed as she smiled at him.

Todd drew his hand back, but his eyes lingered on hers for a moment longer before he shifted his attention back to the bride.

"I've set the room up to look the way you described. I have a table up front set to your specifications," he offered as he led the group toward the front of the room. "We have a DJ if you don't already have one you want to bring. I've arranged catering menus for you to look at, and if you're interested, I'd be happy to take you to the other shops and introduce you around. Pearl is our resident bridal gown expert. Audrey can schedule your bridal party in for hair and makeup for the big day. The florist can design all of your bouquets. And should you need legal counsel, we have that covered, too."

Carol Hanson laughed. "We've heard great things about all the businesses here. Didn't you have a photographer in the building as well?"

"They moved to Kentucky a few months ago. That location has been vacant since."

All the women turned and stared up at Jessie who let out a little laugh as she shook her head. "I'm a photographer. They think I need a studio," she admitted as she looked down at her mother who shrugged a shoulder and smiled at her daughter.

He'd seen his aunt and uncle look at their children and the wives of their children with that *I believe in you* look, just as Carol did with Jessie. But Todd's father didn't bother with such sincerity, and his mother was a piece of work in her own right.

"I'd be happy to show you the space when we're finished if you'd like to look at it," Todd offered.

All eyes were back on Jessie. "That would be lovely. Thank you."

Todd went back to the business at hand—wooing the bride-to-be with all that the *Bridal Mecca* offered.

. . .

As usual, Jessie followed the women who touched every piece of silverware, looked under the tablecloths, checked the glasses for smudges, and even spun on the dance floor. This was the fourth venue this week they had looked at for her sister's wedding, and Jessie was over it.

She loved her sister and her sister's fiancé, but why they had to involve Jessie was beyond her. Shouldn't the bride and groom decide on everything? Why did the bridal party—the women—have to do it all? Jessie didn't care what flowers she had, or the color of the dresses. No matter what her sister put her in it would look hideous anyway. Her athletic build didn't lend itself to elegant dresses.

If she were candid, she'd rather be the one taking the pictures of the day and not be included in the background of each image. Her passion was capturing the surrounding sentiments, not faking a smile while immersed in the festivities.

Maybe they could have one more heart-to-heart about it. It honored her that her sister wanted her to be front and center with her, but Jessie just wasn't comfortable with it.

Now wasn't the time or place to mention it—again. Her sister seemed taken by the location and the women they were meeting in all the quaint shops.

While Todd introduced Carlie to the women in the hair salon, Jessie walked down to the empty shop at the end of the building.

Cupping her hands around her eyes, she looked through the window.

The space would be a nice size for a studio. There was plenty of room to display photos, and it looked like there was a back room where she could stage.

"I have the key if you'd like to go in," Todd said, and Jessie snapped her head up to see him walking toward her.

"It's a nice location."

"Nicely priced too."

Jessie clasped her arms behind her back, which she found she did when she was nervous, but she couldn't help herself. "Are they sold on the venue?" she asked, and Todd smiled.

"I hope so. That's my job, right? Make the venue fit the bride?"

"Is that your job?"

He chuckled as he jingled the keys in his jacket pocket. "I'm filling in for the woman who owns the building. Does it show?"

Jessie shook her head. "You did very well. What's your real job?"

"Cattle rancher."

"Walker Ranch?"

"You know it?"

Tucking her hands into the pockets of her jacket, Jessie shrugged a shoulder. "I've lived in the area most of my life. You don't do that and not run into a Walker or two."

"True. But I don't recall ever seeing you before, and I'd remember."

He was looking her in the eye, and not up and down. That was a first, she thought. Men usually looked at her height and decided she was only a basketball player and nothing more. Well, they wouldn't be wrong. Basketball had paid her way through college and kept her busy on the weekends, but Todd looked into her eyes as if he knew there was more to her.

"Can I look around the space while you finish with my sister?" Jessie asked and watched as Todd pulled the keys from his pocket.

"Take all the time you want." He handed her the keys. "You can bring them back over when you're done, or I'll find you when I'm done with them." He nodded toward the salon.

"I appreciate it."

Todd turned back as Carlie and her party walked out of the salon. They huddled together giggling, including her mother. They were in their element, and Jessie was happy to be unlocking the door to what could be a fresh new start for her. She'd never owned her own business before, and the thought intrigued her immensely. She played it cool when her mother brought it up, but it tickled her inside to think about it.

If she did it, she'd do it on her own. No handouts. Nobody would help her set it up or getting her business. If she would go into business for herself, she would do all the work.

When Jessie slipped the key into the lock, she heard Todd's voice again as he spoke to her sister. Jessie lifted her head and watched them turn the corner with the sexy, out-of-place cowboy.

Working alongside the women they had just met would have its benefits. And, if she got the chance to look at Todd Walker every day, that would be the bonus.

CHAPTER 2

*C*ontract signed, Todd added the information to the email he sent to Lydia every day, keeping her updated on how her business was doing.

After she had checked out of the hospital, feeling as if she'd fully mentally recovered from her ordeal, Lydia had sent for her mother, and the two of them had been vacationing in Hawaii. She wasn't ready to return to Georgia and the daily dealing with people. He could understand that. Todd was used to working on the Walker Ranch and only dealing with his cousins and his uncle. Being in town, among his sisters and his cousins' wives, and the people that came in to see the venue, he'd talked to more people in a few months than he had his entire life.

As he sent off the email, he thought about being surrounded by people. He'd found, to his surprise, he hadn't minded it as much as he'd thought he would. Though, he'd much rather be on a horse riding the pastures in the sunshine. That time would come. The most important thing was to have Lydia healed.

He heard the door open to the reception hall, and not expecting anyone, he jumped up from his chair behind the desk and headed out to see who had come in.

Again, there was no surprise when he saw Phillip Smythe saunter in. He'd become a regular visitor over the past few months, but mostly he was looking for information on Lydia.

"Hey, Phillip. Looks like a storm might move in this afternoon."

With his hat in his hands, Phillip ran his fingers over the brim. "Yeah. You can tell it in the moods of the people. Everyone has a little bite in them today."

And Todd figured Phillip would see that most. Perhaps those were the times when everyone was being pulled over for speeding, and here Todd thought they had a quota to meet.

"Have you heard from Lydia?" Phillip asked, and Todd was grateful he wasn't one to beat around the bush. He wasn't sure he could have continued a conversation about the weather.

"I just sent her an email. I booked another wedding for June."

Phillip nodded. "She's doing okay?"

"She emailed yesterday and said they were doing fine. I think her mother will head back the first of the month, and from the sounds of it, Lydia's ready for that too. She never says when she'll be back, just that things are good."

"Good. Don't tell her I asked. It'll just make her mad."

Todd never offered the information, but from time to time Lydia would ask if Phillip had been in to check on her. When Todd would tell her he'd stopped in, she didn't have a snippy retort. Perhaps she was healing from all things that had once bothered her, including Phillip Smythe.

When the door to the hall opened again, his sister Pearl walked in, and as always, she commanded the room.

"I thought I saw your cruiser outside," she said moving in toward Phillip and pressing a kiss to his cheek.

Pearl was a ray of sunshine wherever she walked, Todd thought. She had a confidence he'd never had, and a professionalism that made her very successful as a bridal consultant.

With her husband Tyson, Lydia's brother, she owned half of

the building that housed the *Bridal Mecca*, a conglomerate of stores that catered to brides. It had been a risky business proposition that had paid off.

"I have a platter of sandwiches over at my store that needs to be eaten," she offered to both of them. "We scheduled a bridal party to come by this morning to choose the dress, and the groom chose someone else. So, there's lots of food."

"I don't…" Phillip began, but Pearl cut off his words just by lifting one of her perfectly manicured fingers.

"You can stop and get a bite to eat. Even if you take it with you." She then turned her attention to Todd. "And you, you'd better come get your share. Maybe take some home for dinner. I'm telling you, I'd planned for a big party."

"I'll be there in a few minutes."

She seemed satisfied when she nodded, and then she took Phillip by the arm and escorted him out of the hall.

It took Todd another ten minutes to add in the information Bethany had sent him about Lydia's other businesses. Her business partners would answer to Bethany, she would answer to Todd, and he would pass on the information to Lydia. He would never understand how one woman could keep that much data in her head—as Lydia must have always done. Every time he looked at a spreadsheet, he swore he was triggering a migraine.

When he heard the door open again, he figured his sister came to pull him away from the desk. "I said I'd be there, didn't I? There is no need to keep pestering me," he said loudly and expected a nasty reply.

"Mr. Walker?" He heard the soft voice ask and could feel the heat fill his cheeks from sheer embarrassment.

Todd rose from behind his desk and walked out to the hall where he found Jessie Hanson standing on the dance floor. She didn't sport the same dress she'd worn that morning when she met him with her sister. She'd pulled her sandy hair back into a ponytail, and she had on a pair of yoga pants and a tank top that showed off her muscular shoulders.

Todd wondered if he'd gasped when he'd seen her. She was mesmerizing.

"I'm very sorry for my greeting," he said as he walked toward her assuming his best business posture and smile. "I had just been talking to my sister."

"It's okay," she said on a laugh and her head dipped as she did so. "I wanted to see if I could look at the space again. If you're busy, I can plan to..."

"I'm not busy at all. Let me get the keys and I'll walk over with you," he offered as he turned back to the office to get the keys and catch his breath.

This woman, whom he'd now seen twice, had his attention. She wasn't dainty or soft, which he had to assume would make most men turn the other way, but he was the opposite. He couldn't help but stare—and that was unprofessional. Surely she'd had enough of that in her life. Women over six feet tall probably didn't get a lot of glances that weren't just fixated on their height.

Retrieving the keys, he turned off the computer monitor and the lights, and closed the door behind him.

"If you don't mind, can we walk through the parking lot and around the building? I just need to make sure everything is being kept up."

"Of course," she agreed, and followed him to the door.

He didn't need to look at anything, and it would take them two minutes longer to walk around the back. But he didn't want to walk past his sister's store and risk his entire family seeing him do so with a woman—a fascinating woman.

CHAPTER 3

She made him nervous. Jessie knew all the signs. He'd tucked his hands in his pockets and was jingling the keys. Todd Walker had asked to walk around the back of the building, she was sure there was a different reason than just checking on the lot. Was he embarrassed to stand next to her?

It wasn't anything new. Her height intimidated every man she had ever encountered, professionally or privately. She'd been five-foot-eight in middle school, two more inches followed in high school. Only boys on the basketball team would ask her to prom. And wasn't it funny, that the smallest of boys were the ones that always had crushes on her?

None of that mattered, it was so long ago. But every time she met someone new, those thoughts crossed her mind. Her height had given her an entire career. It had thrown full scholarships at her feet from notable universities. She rode that basketball train all the way to a bachelor's degree in business. Photography had always been a hobby. Though, it made her a nice income on the side.

She did senior portraits for her sister's friends. A few friends who had gotten married, and couldn't afford a *real* photographer, had scraped up a little money to pay for Jessie to take their pictures. During tournaments, when she wasn't coaching, she would take action shots, and some of them sold.

Now, here she was considering renting a space and making it more than a hobby. If she took this on, it would be a career. It wasn't like she wouldn't use her degree, after all, this would be business. And, when she had majored in business, she wasn't sure what that even meant.

There were other factors, too. Lydia Morgan's businesses were well known in the area. If you could get Lydia to recommend your business, you were golden. She knew everyone. She did business with everyone, and everyone liked her. Even with a reputation like that, Jessie still had gone home and looked up the *Bridal Mecca* just to see what everyone else said about it.

Usually when you looked up a business online, it was full of negative reviews. One thing Jessie had learned over the years was that people who didn't like something spoke much louder than those who did. She was always careful not to base her opinions solely on a review. If she had done that, she never would have tried the Mexican restaurant up the street which was now one of her most favorite places to eat. The *Bridal Mecca*, and all of its independently-owned stores, had nothing but stellar reviews. Audrey's hair salon was one of the most beloved salons in the area. She came across an article where they had gone from four stylists to eight. Perhaps it didn't hurt that Audrey married some hunky movie star, who often frequented her business. But Jessie knew well enough that just having a famous person in your midst didn't speak for the quality of work. The reason Audrey's salon was so popular was because she hired quality stylists.

The reception hall had the most reviews. The one stars came from people not served alcohol. Those were easy enough to see through. One man was angry because they wouldn't serve him after having had six drinks already. By the belligerent language,

Jessie surmised that the man had probably been a liability when he walked into the reception hall.

All the other reviews were stellar. And, all the other reviews mentioned Lydia Morgan by name. If you booked your social event in her reception hall, you were not disappointed. She hoped that would be the case for her sister. She and her mother had had nothing but good things to say about Todd and everyone they had met.

Todd's other sister, Pearl, owned the bridal shop. She'd had many of her friends buy dresses from Pearl. She supposed, when the day came, she too would choose Pearl. The store was known for being well-stocked, well decorated, and had fair prices.

There was the flower store. She'd ordered a few pieces from there and had them delivered to her mother occasionally. They'd never disappointed.

Jessie hadn't been in the Italian store. Perhaps before she left today she would stop in. Having looked through the window, she knew there was a set of wine glasses she wanted to look closer at.

As they turned the corner, Jessie glanced at the small space at the end of the building. There was a small sign in the window that said Ella Mills-Walker Attorney at Law.

"Are you related to the attorney?" She asked as Todd fished the keys from his pocket.

"Of course. Ella just married my cousin, Gerald."

"It seems like this corner of town has everything a blushing bride would need for her wedding."

Todd stuck the key in the lock and turned it. "That would be their business model. And, it seems to work. Rarely does Pearl sell a dress, and the bride does not buy flowers, have her hair done, or book the reception in Lydia's hall. Oh, and my other cousin's wife, she's the caterer."

"Susan?" She asked as Todd pushed open the door.

"You've met Susan?"

Jessie nodded as Todd turned on the lights. "She catered a

bridal shower for one of my sister's other friends. She's the one that told us about all these businesses. She's the one that sold us on the reception hall." She laughed. "Us. As if I had anything to do with any of the decisions made today."

Todd turned to her and smiled. "It seems as if your mom and sister had that all planned out."

"They did. I'm not sure why they dragged me along. Maybe it was fate. I was supposed to see this space."

Todd looked around the room. "It sure doesn't look like much, does it?"

"I suppose that depends on who's doing the looking. You see an empty space."

"A dirty, empty space. Seriously, did that photographer move out and leave dust?"

Jessie laughed. "Main road. Cars kick up dust." She shrugged. "No, I see something bigger. I see light colors on the walls out here. I don't know if I would say white, or if I might want to go more cream. Portraits in the window." She opened her arms as if to direct his attention in front of them. "A sofa, a couple chairs, and a coffee table filled with books of portraits."

Jessie took a few more steps into the room and faced the wall. "I would cover that wall with baby portraits and young children." She turned to the next wall. "Over here I would put senior portraits and engagement pictures." She turned to the final wall. "Over here I would showcase weddings and big families. I really need to decide if weddings are something I want to throw myself into."

"You're not sure about weddings?"

Jessie turned back toward Todd. "I am sure you could ask your sisters about this. But every little girl has their wedding plan from the time they are five years old. I'm just not sure I want to be the person in charge of capturing that image."

Todd tucked his hands into his front pockets and rocked back on his heels. "Did you plan your wedding at five?"

Jessie shook her head. "I don't think I did. I was too busy outside being a tomboy. I would have much rather been playing flag football, swimming, or shooting layups in the driveway. I can't say I ever gave any thought to a wedding."

"Ever?"

Jessie clasped her arms behind her. "Ever."

CHAPTER 4

Todd had remembered Pearl and Audrey both playing bride when they were younger. It had been his brother, Jake, and his duty to always mess up whatever they had designed to play wedding. Looking back on it, it wasn't a very nice thing to do, but, brothers would be brothers.

He hadn't spent too much time with his sisters growing up anyway, not enough time to know if they planned every detail or which parts of those details had been executed in their own weddings. Pearl had eloped. How ironic that was, he thought. The woman who designed all the most beautiful weddings, didn't even have one. But that was the way she had wanted it.

Had he ever given any thought to his own wedding?

Todd watched Jessie walk around the space stopping here and there as if she were imagining other items on walls.

What kind of wedding would he and Jessie have?

It was such a ridiculous thought that he laughed out loud.

Jessie turned with a quizzical look. "What's so funny?"

"Just your comment about girls planning their wedding since they were five. I was just thinking of how many times my sisters played wedding and my brother and I ruined it."

"I am fairly sure my brother would've done the same thing. I may have to ask my sister, maybe he did."

"Will your brother be in the wedding as well?" Todd asked, walking toward Jessie at the back of the store.

Her gaze dropped to the floor, and she shook her head before looking back up at him. "He was hit on his bicycle when he was thirteen. He died at the hospital three days later."

Todd felt his heart stop. "I'm so sorry."

"Thank you. We lost him physically that day, but there is a little girl—well not little anymore—who lived because she got his heart and another little boy got his kidney. He gave life to others who would not have had any quality of life or length of life."

Todd would not consider himself a sappy man. Tears did not come often. However, he was sure he was choking on emotion when he said, "That's beautiful."

"It is beautiful. My mom and dad almost got divorced after that. Losing a child is something I can't even fathom. Losing a brother was hard enough."

"How old were you?"

"Eleven," she answered quickly and then turned toward the back of the empty store. "I assume that Lydia and your sister wouldn't mind if we put up another wall?"

"I would assume that would be okay. I can go get Pearl and we can ask her. In fact, I know that she has nothing on her schedule right now. She had a bride cancel."

"Why would a bride cancel?"

"Fiancé chose someone else."

"Ouch," Jessie winced.

The door behind him opened and both of them turned to see Pearl walking in. "I didn't know you were showing the property. I thought the lights just got left on."

Pearl walked right to them, again with that air of profession-alism. She held out her hand to Jessie. "Pearl Morgan, Todd's sister."

"Jessie Hanson, sister of a bride I think you met this morning."

"Carlie? And your mother is Carol?"

Jessie smiled. "That's them."

"I have an appointment set with them for next week. Your sister is going to come in and look at dresses. I hope you'll join her."

"I'm sure she'll want me there."

"So," Pearl said as she looked around the room. "What are we doing here?"

Todd moved in closer to his sister. "Ms. Hanson is a photographer. She was looking at the space. Perhaps as the landlord, you can give her more information than I can."

And with that, his sister took over the showing.

AFTER HALF AN HOUR WITH PEARL, Jessie was sold on the property. That morning she had woken up irritated that her sister was making her go to look at venues. There had not been a thought in her mind she'd be going into business for herself.

Pearl had given her all the specifics. She knew the amount of the lease, utilities, and flow of people. Jessie was brought up to date on improvements, and the other businesses, and how they worked together.

Jessie spun one more time around in the space taking it in. She had taken a handful of photos on her phone, to show them to her family.

Pearl had given her the key to lock up and told her to take a few minutes in the space by herself. No one could ever decide on something while a stranger stood over their shoulder, she had told her.

It felt comfortable. Almost too comfortable.

Could she do this?

Did she want to do this?

She understood basketball, and coaching, and the politics

behind it. She had a degree in business. The photographs she had taken were all good, in her opinion. But could she make a living at it? She couldn't keep her job now, even though it meant nothing to her. If she were going to do this, she had to go all in, and weddings were a must. The women she was surrounding herself with were catering to the bridal community, and it was the right decision to do the same.

She hadn't been planning for it. So, there wasn't any nest egg set aside for it. She could ask her parents for some money, or take out a loan at the bank. Either of those options would be a last resort. Jessie was the kind of woman who believed in doing everything herself.

Jessie took a moment and inhaled a deep breath before she tightened her ponytail. This was the craziest thought she'd ever had, and it felt right. She wanted to do this. Honestly, if she was as good as she thought, she had other businesses that would feed her clientele. How could she go wrong?

Jessie walked to the door and turned off the light switch. Again, she looked around the now darkened space. Every day, she thought. Every day she can walk through this door and turn on and off that light. It would be hers. All decisions would be hers.

She shut the door and turned the key in the lock.

Pearl had invited her over to have a sandwich at her bridal shop. Jessie had decided to do just that. She would go to Pearl's store, have a sandwich, and make her decision. Because, it was her decision and no one else's.

As she left the empty space to walk toward Pearl's store, she turned and ran right into Todd, and their foreheads smacked together.

His hands came to her arms to steady her. "I didn't realize I was that quiet. I thought you saw me."

"I think I was deep in thought," she said rubbing her forehead. Then, she noticed that they stood eye to eye, and that his eyes

were deep blue. It was nice to nearly look a man right in the eye
—to actually look up into his eyes.

"Where are you headed? Over to my sister's?" he asked.

"I was. She said she had sandwiches."

Todd laughed as he dropped his hands. "She does. And be
warned, she's going to ask you to take some of them home with
you."

That earned a laugh of her own, and she walked side-by-side
with Todd Walker down the street in front of the building that
she was very convinced she would call home.

CHAPTER 5

The moment they walked through the door of Pearl's bridal shop, Todd noticed the grin on his sister's face. She'd always been a bit too romantic, he thought. He knew, just from her expression, that his walking in with Jessie had set his sister's mind whirling. It would be as ridiculous for Pearl to think about their wedding as it had been for him to wonder what kind of wedding Jessie would want.

Pearl moved toward them and quickly took Jessie's hand in hers. "I'm so glad you came by," she said as she pulled her to the other room. "This doesn't happen often, but when it does, I have to call in the troops."

Todd watched as Jessie's eyes grew big when she saw the platters of sandwiches.

"Do your brides usually do this kind of thing? I mean the food and all?"

"Of course. We make it a big event. Picking out the dress is huge."

"Did you book my sister for one of these?"

Humor lit in Pearl's eyes. "I did. She opted to have more of a high tea. So there won't be this much food, and it will be a little more elegant."

"Which means she's going to want all of us to be here?"

Pearl turned toward Jessie. "You're not enjoying the process of the wedding planning?"

Jessie shrugged. "It's not my wedding. I will go along with whatever my sister wants, of course. But I would much rather be behind the camera than displayed in some pastel dress."

"I do have a way with brides. If you really feel that way, I could talk to your sister on your behalf. Making it sound as if I, an outsider, think it's a good idea."

"Are you kidding? You can do that? You would do that?"

"I've seen enough weddings go sour when someone doesn't want to be in it. Now, no doubt her day will be perfect with or without you in the bridal party, and I don't think you would ruin her day, but if she knew you were happy, she would be happy."

Todd watched as the smile formed on Jessie's lips. "I would be eternally grateful to you."

"Then I will mention it to her when I talked to her on the phone next week. Now, come get some food. I want to hear all about your photography."

Todd realized he could sit and watch his sister work her magic all day long. He'd been there when she talked to brides, when she talked down future mothers-in-law, and when she had to handle a meddling bridesmaid. It was no wonder his sister and her sister-in-law Lydia were so successful in their businesses. They truly believed in what they did, and it showed.

Jessie was sitting next to Pearl on the sofa, eating sandwiches, and laughing. But it was when he heard her say, "I think I would like to lease the space for a photography studio," that he knew his entire life was about to change. This woman, this attention-capturing woman, would be around every day.

Pearl looked up at him. "Are you not going to join us?"

"Oh, yeah," he stammered. "Can I get a Coke out of your fridge?"

"When have you ever asked?" Pearl laughed.

Todd started for the back room and turned back to Jessie. "Can I get you a Coke?"

"No, thank you. I don't do sugar often."

"How about water?"

"That would be fantastic."

Todd nodded and disappeared into the next room.

The thought that he would like to ask Jessie to have dinner with him bounced around in his head. However, maybe that wasn't a very good idea. If she was in fact going to sign a lease to work in the building, maybe he'd better let this little puppy crush diffuse. She was mesmerizing, beautiful, and interesting. He'd like to get to know her more, and he supposed he would get to if they worked close by. Maybe he had been spending too much time at the *Bridal Mecca*. Suddenly he had stars in his eyes for the first interesting woman that had walked through the door in months. Maybe it was that she was single, and all the women he did business with were usually getting married. No, Jessie was different. There was just something about her he couldn't put his finger on. He'd let this little infatuation simmer. No doubt Lydia would be back soon, and then he would be back at the ranch. They were all in a transition stage, and it wouldn't last much longer.

JESSIE WAS sure she was making the right decision. Sitting on Pearl's sofa, eating sandwiches, and talking bridal parties, made her very comfortable.

She was as close to her sister as sisters could get, but in just a few minutes she felt as if she had just adopted another sister.

Pearl was full of wisdom, and business sense. Oh, the things that Jessie could learn from her. Her energy was infectious. All Jessie could hope was that she would be as successful in her business as Pearl seemed to be in hers. And, with the networking between all the businesses, they almost guaranteed clientele.

And then there was Todd Walker, she thought as he came from the back room with a Coke in one hand and a bottle of water in the other. Since the moment she had met him that morning, he had been on her mind. Maybe she had hit her head against his harder than she thought. The thought humored her, so she bit into her sandwich.

Todd handed her the bottle of water. "Thank you."

"My pleasure," he said as he sat on the arm of the sofa.

Pearl turned to him. "Remove your ass from the arm of the sofa and put it in the seat of that chair," she demanded, and he rolled his eyes.

Oh, God, that had been adorable. Did Pearl have this kind of power over everyone? Jessie wondered how she could get that, too.

Pearl turned toward her. "So what do you say we talk some business? Are you interested in the space?"

Jessie set her sandwich on the small table and folded her hands in her lap. "I have never made a decision this big in my life."

"All I can say is that you're in the right place. The *Bridal Mecca* is filled with entrepreneurial women who support each other. Yes, we're all family, mostly, but we have a community. We would all do everything we could to make sure you succeeded," Pearl offered.

Jessie could feel the tears stinging the back of her eyes, and she fought them down, willing them not surface. "That is generous of you." She sucked in a deep breath and let it out slowly. "My mom and my sister have been trying to talk me into this for years. I think I want to take the space."

Pearl clapped her hands together and smiled. "I think you made the right decision." She turned toward Todd. "Third drawer of the black filing cabinet in Lydia's office, that's where the leases are. Why don't you go get one and bring it back? Let's get this fine woman set up in business."

CHAPTER 6

*J*essie sat in her car outside the *Bridal Mecca*. She had already been sitting there twenty minutes with a stupid grin on her face. On the seat next to her lay the lease she had just signed. It was official. She was a business owner.

Running through her mind were all the things she wanted to accomplish in this new business, and the list of things she needed to do to get started. First, she needed a name for her company. Second, she needed to get a business license. And the list went on with tax licenses, bank accounts, insurance, and equipment.

She rested back against the headrest and closed her eyes. What had she done?

Surely, if she walked back into the bridal shop, Pearl would allow her to rip up the lease. But that wasn't what she wanted. Never in her life had Jessie turned away from a challenge. This was just another game. This was the tip-off, first quarter. Now all she had to do was take the ball to the other end and slam dunk it. Putting it into terms she understood made it a little less scary.

Determined she didn't want to take any handouts from her family, she toyed with the thought of not telling them what she had done until she had completed all the steps. Then again, she was just too excited. Seriously, this called for a celebration.

Jessie picked up her phone from the cubby where she kept it while she drove. She scrolled through to her messages and found Aspen's name. No doubt her best friend in the entire world would want to come and celebrate Jessie's new adventure. But just as Jessie started to type in the text, she remembered that Aspen, and her current flavor of the month, had driven down to Destin for the week.

It would completely defeat the purpose of holding out information from her family if she were to invite them to celebrate.

She scrolled through her contacts, and considered each of her weekend teammates, but none of their names resonated with her celebration.

It was then that somebody knocked on the window, startling her, and causing her to throw her phone. When she looked up, Todd Walker was standing at the window looking in at her, with his hands up in surrender.

Jessie rolled down the passenger side window. "You scared the hell out of me."

"I swear to you, I'm not some kind of stalker. I didn't mean to startle you again."

She nearly asked what the 'again' was about, then she remembered running right into him. "It's okay. I rarely startle so easily."

"You looked as though you were deep in thought."

"I was."

Todd rested his arms on the car door and leaned in. "Are you okay? You've been sitting here for quite a while."

Jessie smiled. "I'm taking it in. Making some mental lists. I've never done anything like this. I'm a little freaked out."

The smile that formed on Todd's lips had Jessie's insides turning to mush. He was easy with that southern charm, something Jessie had always been a sucker for.

"You seem to me to be a woman who lets nothing stand in her

way. I have no doubt you will be the most successful photographer in Georgia."

She found that she nearly sighed, but kept it in. "You have no idea what kind of photographer I am."

"No, but I'm a good judge of character."

"Thank you." She looked down at the lease and the seat and then back up to Todd. "I was thinking I needed to celebrate, but I'm not ready to tell my parents and sister what I've done yet."

"Why not? Weren't they the ones urging you to look into it?"

"Yes. But I also know they're going to want to help me. Not necessarily physically, but they'll step in when I need help. I know that my mom and dad have money set aside for things like this, you know, to help me out."

Todd's brows drew together. "And you don't want to?"

"I've never done anything in my life that I didn't do on my own. Rumor has it, I even potty-trained myself."

That caused him to chuckle. "Well, coming from parents who won't even lift a finger for me, I have to say you are one lucky woman. However, I like your determination. It always feels better when you do something on your own."

She felt her own smile tugging at her cheeks. "Exactly. There is nothing better than knowing there is a safety net, and never needing to use it."

"Like I said, I think you'll be the most successful photographer in Georgia."

Jessie realized it was easy to get lost in those blue eyes looking back at her. Then she thought, it was a day of spontaneity. "Would you like to go out for a drink? To celebrate my lease? To celebrate your success in renting the open space?"

The smile slipped from tough lips, and that told her everything she needed to know.

He stepped back and opened the car door. "You drive, I'll buy."

It wasn't what she had expected, and her heart did a little

flutter in her chest. Quickly, she moved the lease from the passenger seat and tucked it into the glove box.

Todd climbed in the car and put on his seatbelt. "Do you like Mexican food?"

"One of my favorites."

"Couple of blocks over. Lydia, my sister's business partner, is an owner in a brewery, and they sell their beer there. We can't go wrong."

"It sounds like a party to me."

Jessie started the engine and pulled away from the curb.

TODD LISTENED to Garth Brooks on the radio, as the warm Georgia air blew through Jessie's car. He had four contracts sitting on his desk that needed his attention, a liquor order that was due tomorrow morning, and a handful of lightbulbs that needed changing in the reception hall. The last thing he should do was leave it all to go to dinner with this woman who'd had his attention all day.

But he couldn't help himself.

It didn't seem to be enough that he would work a few hundred feet away from her every day. Well, that was until Lydia came back.

Since the minute Jessie Hanson walked into the reception hall with her mother and sister, his mind had been on getting to know her better.

"What made you get into photography?" he asked as Jessie turned the corner at the light.

"I don't know. Something I've done my entire life. I bought my first camera when I was eight, with birthday money. It was digital. I filled up the memory card, and my dad loaded them on his computer. I got to choose the ten I liked the most, and he sent them to have them printed."

"What was the subject of those pictures?"

Just took a big breath and let it out with a laugh. "Would you be surprised if I told you they were all obscure pictures of a basketball?"

Now Todd laughed. "It's a big part of your life, isn't it?"

"Since the moment I could walk. My dad played on a rec league, so on Wednesday nights and Sunday mornings we were court side. They had me on a rec league by the time I was four. I guess it goes full-circle. Now I'm the one playing on Sundays and they are courtside."

"I think that's awesome. I played football up through high school. Rode my bike to practice. Rode my bike home. Usually did the same after games. I'm not sure my dad ever saw a game. My brother races cars, and the only time my dad shows up to the track is when he bets against him."

He wasn't sure what made him throw his family's past out there like that. His relationship with his father wasn't something that controlled his life. His mother kept to herself. He always knew that was why he worked out at the ranch with his uncle and his cousins. Now that was a real family.

"I think it's sad when parents miss out on things. I'm sure that when you are a parent, you won't be like that."

"You can bet on it. My kids will be so tired of me, if I ever have kids, that they'll wish I didn't show up."

Jessie laughed as she pulled into the parking lot of the restaurant. "Blessed with parents that show up to everything, I can guarantee children never tire of it." She turned off the engine and unbuckled her seatbelt. "Regardless of who was on the sidelines, I saw how you acted with your sister. Maybe your dad and your mom weren't there, but it's easy to see you have a tight-knit family."

There were times Todd had to remind himself of that. He and Jake always had each other's backs. And when it came to his sisters, though they had another mother, Audrey and Pearl were equally by his side. Even though it took until they were adults for

Bethany to become part of their lives, she too was as important to him. Jessie was right, it didn't matter who'd showed up then, it mattered who was there now. The five of them were a force to be reckoned with if anyone messed with one of them. Well, he thought he was here to celebrate her accomplishments, but now he felt like maybe he was celebrating his own.

CHAPTER 7

Todd hadn't considered that it was Saturday afternoon, and the restaurant already had a waiting list.

"I don't mind waiting," Jessie said as the hostess jotted down Todd's name. "Why don't we go get a beer from the bar. You can tell me which one is Lydia's. I love a good craft beer."

"So, which beer is it?" Jessie asked.

Todd looked at the small menu on the bar. He scanned the names and pointed to one. "It's this one. There's a light one and a stout one."

"I'll take the stout. I'm no wimpy beer drinker," Jessie noted with a smile.

No, he wouldn't take her for a light beer drinker at all. Something told him that Jessie Hanson lived life to the fullest, and that included stout beers.

He ordered two of the darker beers and handed one to her when the bartender slid them across the bar. "Here's to brand-new beginnings," he offered as he tapped his glass to hers.

Jessie nodded and blew out a breath. "To new beginnings. Brand-new businesses, and brand-new friendships."

She took a long sip from her beer, and Todd watched. Friendship. He hadn't realized it until today, but he desperately needed a friend. And what better timing, he thought. A long-legged blonde with an athletic build, a quest to do things on her own, and a love of stout beer had walked into his life that morning. Perhaps someone above was watching out for him. At least while he was in charge of Lydia's businesses, and he had to stay in town more often, it would be nice to have a friend nearby. Considering that Jessie would be right around the corner, perhaps he'd use the opportunity to get to know her even better.

"So when do you play basketball again?" he asked as they walked out to the patio to wait for their table.

"I play on Sunday evenings. Just over at the Y."

"That's a co-ed league," he said, and Jessie lowered her beer and smiled.

"How do you know that?"

"I work out there when I'm in town. I've watched from the window a few times."

"Why don't you plan to be working out tomorrow evening? The game starts at six. Maybe you could happen by the window again," she offered as she lifted her drink to her lips and sipped.

And just like that he would see her again tomorrow, he decided.

"I think I might just do that."

THEY SAT in a booth in the back corner of the restaurant, one on each side of the table. Jessie had indulged in a second beer, which wasn't normal for her, but then again, the entire day had been a little off kilter.

She'd get up early tomorrow morning and go for a longer run, she decided, as the waitress delivered her fajita platter. Todd had opted for a smothered burrito plate, which had never been her style. Food covered in any kind of gravy, as she considered it, wasn't worth eating.

They talked about the *Bridal Mecca*, and how it had come to be. Todd filled her in on the once brutal feud between the Walkers and the Morgans, and found humor in the fact that his sister had married Tyson Morgan and gone into business with his sister.

"People just need to open their eyes," she said, taking her fork and eating the chicken right off the skillet on which they had served it to avoid putting it into a tortilla. She was having enough carbs with the beer. "The fights of our grandparents, and great-grandparents, don't have to continue to be our own. It's a glorious time we live in right now. Women are becoming more equal to men. And men are finding out they don't have to be so macho."

She watched Todd chew his bottom lip as he pulled his fork from the silverware bundle. "I don't know if my masculinity just took a hit or not."

"I didn't mean men weren't men, I just think they're open to being more emotional, more into themselves."

Todd cut into his burrito and took the first bite. "My father would probably slap me on the back of the head if I agreed with you, but he's not here."

"So you agree with me?"

"I probably wouldn't have five years ago. I worked on a ranch full of men. Everyone was single. But now, now that everyone in my family is married, and some of them have kids. I see a whole new side to these people."

Jessie sat back in the booth and picked up her beer. "And what about you? Where do you fall on the idea of women being equal?"

"This is very dangerous territory," he sat back against his booth and took a sip of his beer. "Honestly, I think women are superior to men. They create life, they nurture life, and dammit, in my world, they run all the businesses." He laughed.

"You are surrounded by some of the strongest women I think I've ever met."

"Seriously. Both of my sisters and all the wives of my cousins are in business. Hell, my sister-in-law drives race cars."

"Now she's a freaking badass," Jessie admitted as she set her beer down and scooped up another forkful of veggies.

"Don't I know it? She scares the hell out of me."

That sent a ripple of laughter through Jessie and she leaned in on her elbows. "I promise to never let her know that."

"I'm sure she knows it. I just keep her on my good side."

The conversation continued, just like that. Never in Jessie's entire life had she been so comfortable with a man she had just met. It would be nice to see him every day, she considered, as he told her about his childhood and his father being in and out of his life. When she'd finished her meal, she sat back, beer in hand, and watched him as he talked about his sisters and how they were always a shining light in his life as he grew up, even though they never lived in the same house.

Her heart sank when he talked about Bethany and her growing up in Hollywood with her washed-up actress mother who died from an overdose. What an eclectic family, Jessie thought, as she listened. Bethany had gone through rehab herself and married an author. Pearl had married a Morgan, and Audrey had married one of the most famous actors in Hollywood. Jessie hoped that Gregory Bishop was a regular at the *Bridal Mecca*. Wouldn't her friends be envious of her meeting him?

Todd talked about his brother, the race car driver, and his badass wife, Missy. He laughed when he told her about how much they'd hated each other, only to find true love.

Jessie had to believe it when his eyes lit, that he believed in true love and that opposites attract.

Did she believe in it? She'd never much been caught up in finding the right person or dating much. She just didn't have time for it. Okay, she didn't make time for it. She was happy doing her own thing. But being with Todd was comfortable. It wasn't a date, just two people who did some business together having a bite to eat, but she liked it. Maybe he would show up to watch her play tomorrow, and wouldn't that be interesting? She'd never had a man purposefully attend a game—then again, she had only told him to work out and watch through the window.

When her beer was empty, she set the glass on the table, a little sad that the night was about to end. Tomorrow offered a lot of possibilities though.

CHAPTER 8

It was just past seven Sunday morning when Jessie parked her car in front of her parents' house and retrieved the box of bagels from the passenger seat. She should have made it her first stop after she'd signed the lease on her new studio, but she'd chosen dinner with Todd Walker instead, and hadn't that had her mind racing all night?

Her mother had opened the door, still in her robe, before Jessie even climbed out of the car.

"What a nice surprise. You should have told us you were coming over," her mother held open the screen door and waited for her to ascend the front steps.

"I'm not interrupting anything, am I?"

"Heavens no. I just would have gotten dressed. That's all." She kissed Jessie on the cheek and Jessie could smell the fresh mint of her mother's toothpaste.

"I guess I should have let you know I was coming," she said, sniffing the aroma of coffee in the air. "Did you eat already?"

"Nope. Happy to see you came with that." Her mother nodded to the box in her hand. "C'mon. Daddy is at the table with his paper."

Jessie followed her mother to the kitchen and smiled when she saw her father sitting right where her mother had told her he would be. His favorite coffee mug sat on the table as he managed the enormous paper in front of him. He looked over the top and waited for her to kiss him on the cheek.

"Good morning, Daddy."

"Nice surprise," he said as he folded the paper and set it next to his coffee. "To what do we owe the pleasure so early?"

Jessie set the box of bagels on the table and pulled out a chair as her mother filled two coffee mugs and carried them to the table.

"I've been up for hours. Took an early run. I went out to eat with Todd Walker last night, and we tried one of the stout beers that's produced by a company Lydia Morgan owns."

She'd seen the glances shift between her parents when she'd mentioned dinner with Todd Walker. Jessie was just going to continue on and see where the conversation went.

"I figured I needed to get up and running to account for the carbs in the beers," she laughed as she opened the bagel box and took out an everything bagel and the regular cream cheese.

Her father folded up his paper and set it to the side before reaching into the box himself.

"Mom tells me y'all met Todd Walker yesterday when you booked your sister's reception."

Jessie nodded as she bit down on her bagel. "Yep. Nice guy."

Now her mother reached for a bagel and stood to take it to the toaster and retrieve the butter from the refrigerator. "You went to dinner with him?" she asked as she waited for her bagel to toast.

And now they were into the conversation.

"I went back to the *Bridal Mecca* to look at that space again," she said before picking up her coffee and taking a sip. "I wanted to spend a few more moments there and look around."

Again, her parents exchanged glances.

Jessie heard the toaster pop out her mother's bagel and watched as she carried it back to the table, on a plate, with the butter tub in her other hand.

"You went back and looked again?" her mother asked. "What did you think this time?"

"I signed a lease on the space."

Her father slapped a congratulatory hand on hers, and her mother stood and kissed her on the cheek. "I think that's fantastic. I knew that spot would be good for you. Oh, it's so cute, Fred," she said to her father. "Tell me what you're thinking of doing there."

Jessie chuckled as she sipped her coffee. "I figure I'll get started, and then I'll find a niche. The obvious thing to do is weddings, but I've only done weddings for friends. But it fits into the motif of the businesses that surround me. If I market this correctly, I start with engagements, and then do their weddings. In a few years I have newborn portraits and then family portraits. Eventually that moves to senior pictures, and the cycle starts all over, right?"

Her mother's smiled peeked out from behind her bagel as she took a bite. "I'm very excited for you."

Jessie's father crossed his legs and eased back in his chair. "We want to help you," he offered, and Jessie shook her head.

"I know that you do. I know you've set aside savings for this, and I'm very appreciative, but I want to make this happen on my own."

Her mother wiped her mouth with a napkin. "Jessie, we're paying for your sister's wedding, we've helped her get started with the new house and her education. We want to..."

"Hold on to it for me," she said reaching her hand to cover her mother's. "Invest it. I'm perfectly fine if you spend it on yourselves. But I can do this. I need to do this. If something comes up, then I know you'll have my back."

Letting out a sigh, her mother wiped a tear from her eyes. "Fred, she's just like you. So wonderfully stubborn."

Her father laughed. "She says that's a wonderful trait when it's about you, but I don't think she likes it usually."

They had a good laugh about that, and by the time Jessie left her parents' house, she felt good about the choices she'd made.

There was a lot of planning that needed to happen in the next month. She needed licenses, insurance, furniture, props, samples, and clients.

As she sat in her car at a stoplight just down the street from the *Bridal Mecca*, the list in her head grew longer and longer. Maybe she should have taken her parents' generosity.

No. She knew what she wanted and how she wanted it. If she were to make it in business, she would do it on her own.

Instead of going toward her new studio, as she'd planned to do, she headed home. There was a great need stirring inside of her to write down everything she needed to do. Starting bright and early on Monday morning Jessie would build her own empire among the women of the Walker family. That was something to be very proud of.

CHAPTER 9

There was a need to gather eggs, muck out a horse stall, and fix a fence with Eric. Todd had spent the past few months in town, but once in a while he needed to get his boots dirty and let the sun shine down on his neck.

"You seem like you have a lot on your mind," Eric said as he shoveled in the stall next to Todd.

"Every day," he said with a laugh. "I worry about Lydia. Just when I think she might be ready to come home, she changes her mind. I've booked the hall for months, signed on a new lease on that empty spot in the building, and then I had dinner with the new tenant."

Todd noticed the noise from the other stall had stopped, and he looked up to see Eric, arms propped up on the dividing wall, looking down at him.

"That's what's on your mind. You signed a lease with a woman and then took her dinner?"

"You're a genius how you figured that out," Todd offered as he continued to shovel. "She's a nice gal. Plays basketball. Takes pictures."

"What kind of pictures?"

The noise in the other stall had begun again, and Todd was more at ease if they could have their heart to heart over the smell of horse crap as they shoveled.

"I suppose she'll do wedding pictures. Why wouldn't she? Her sister is the one I rented the hall to for her wedding."

"Hanson?"

"Yeah." Todd stopped shoveling and waited for Eric to appear over the wall again.

"Susan booked the catering. I remembered the family though. The sister getting married is older, right?"

Todd shrugged his shoulders. "I have no idea. I know they had a brother."

"Freddie." Eric leaned in over the wall again. "Died when he was a kid."

"How do you know them?"

"I remember the tragedy of it." He took off his hat and ran his hand over his hair before replacing his hat.

"She told me about it. I guess I should count my blessings more often. I have all of you and my siblings. Interesting how sound families can go through tragedy and come out strong, and some of us carry our own baggage for nothing."

He noticed that Eric had disappeared from the wall, and a moment later a pile of hay and the foulness of horse crap flew over the wall and into the stall Todd was mucking out.

"What in the hell are you doing?" He stepped back and heard the laughter from Eric.

"You're not your dad and never have been. Pull your head out of your ass and realize that all five of you are worth more than your parts. Now finish this so I can go do something else. I'm tired of smelling horse shit."

It was nearly four-thirty when Todd drove away from Walker Ranch. He'd showered before he left, even though he was headed to the Y to work out.

The very thought of it brought a smile to his face. He would happen by the gym at six o'clock, just as Jessie had suggested he do. Maybe he could convince her to go out for a celebratory drink after. No doubt she'd win her game—he assumed.

He took time to do a few laps in the pool before hitting the weight room. The local football team seemed to have dibs on most of the benches, but he managed a few sets worked in before giving up and heading to the machines.

In his experience, the retired population usually dominated the machines, and they were ruthless when you sat just a moment too long between sets. But alas, that was the price you paid for not shelling out big bucks on a meat-market gym instead.

Todd kept his eye on the clock. When it was time, he headed to the locker room, showered, and changed before happening by the window to the gym at six-ten.

A chill zipped down his spine when he saw her. She was up against a man, who towered over her, for the tip-off. As the ball flew up, she leapt from the ground, and she managed the ball before he did. The sound of shoes against the wooden floor signaled that the play was moving. The ball moved from one player to another, with Jessie getting the ball at the net and jumping for the layup, just as the taller man jumped to bat it down. He succeeded, but the ball came back at Jessie's face. She fell to the floor, and the man fell on top of her.

Todd didn't remember thinking about it at all. He ran into the gym and right out onto the floor where they had gathered around her. A man with a big red cross on his shirt was down next to her.

Her face was covered in blood, and the man was pressing a rag to her nose.

She saw him through the crowd, and the smile lit in her eyes, even though her mouth was covered.

"Jessie, I'm so sorry," the big man was kneeling down next to her. "I can't believe I knocked you like that."

"I'm fine, Finn," she mumbled from beneath the towel. "Let me up, I'll be okay in a bit."

They all helped her to her feet, and another employee hurried out to the court to clean and sanitize the floor as they helped Jessie to the bench.

Just as quickly as Jessie had gone down, the game resumed.

"Nice time to show up for a game, huh?" she said as she laughed, the towel still pressed to her nose while the medic worked on getting an ice pack prepared.

"Are you okay? That scared the hell out of me."

"Finn is just a clod. He would never have hurt me on purpose. Tweaked my knee a little," she said as the medic placed the icepack on the knee Finn had landed on.

The medic took another minute to make sure she was okay, before handing her a wipe for her face.

"Do you have your phone?" she asked Todd.

"Sure."

"Open the camera and hold it up. I want to make sure I get this all off my face."

He did as she asked, and she wiped away the blood that had coated her. Now she looked just as she had, only her nose was swollen and red, but that seemed to be okay with her.

"You sticking around for the rest of the game?" she asked, throwing the wipe into the small trash can between the benches.

"You're going to keep playing?"

"Game must go on, right?" she offered as she watched the play on the court.

"Right. Yeah, I'll stay. Can I take you out for a drink after?"

She turned and looked up at him standing next to her. "Finn owes me one for messing up my face. But you should go with us. Maybe when they all leave, we can have our own drink."

Todd nodded. There was something about this woman that intrigued him. "I'll wait around for you."

CHAPTER 10

Jessie had given Todd directions to the bar before she headed to the locker room to shower.

One look in the mirror and she nearly cried.

Her nose was already turning purple, and her right eye was going to be bruised too. During it all she must have bitten her lip, because that was tender and had a fresh cut.

As per the norm, Finn felt worse about it than she did. It wasn't the first time he'd run her over. It wouldn't be the last.

The man stood nearly six-eight, and he just didn't have control over his long body. He was also nearly sixty, so trying to keep up with all the thirty-year-olds, that commanded some respect. And that was what Jessie had for the man. Nothing but respect.

By the time she'd pulled up to the bar, everyone was there. As she stepped out of her car, she saw Todd walking toward her.

"I thought you'd be inside," she said tucking her phone and wallet into her pocket.

"I didn't want to go in without you. I was worried about you."

Jessie shrugged. "This is normal. You'll see me like this again. People think basketball is easy, but you still get hurt. I can't even tell you how many ankle braces I own because I've rolled my ankle. I've dislocated my knee three times. Oh, and jammed fingers—I've lost count."

"And you'll show up next Sunday to do it all over again?"

"Bet your ass I will." She took a bold step toward him. "Will you show up next Sunday to watch?"

He blinked hard and nodded. "Every Sunday."

And that was what she'd wanted to hear.

Jessie's drink was waiting for her when she walked into the bar. Finn shook his head as he handed it to her. "One of these days you're going to come up from the floor and sock me in the nose."

She lifted on her toes, and he bent down, so she could kiss him on the cheek. "Never—ever. You keep showing up to knock me down, and I'll keep getting up so you'll buy me a beer."

Jessie introduced Todd to the others and then ordered a plate of nachos. Over the next hour, one by one the other players left the bar or were joined by their families and escorted to the adjoining restaurant to eat. When Finn called it a night, he kissed Jessie on the top of the head and shook Todd's hand.

"He's a good guy," Todd said as he pulled a nacho from the plate.

"Great guy. He was on scene when my brother got hit. I think that's why it bothers him so much when I'm the one that goes down under him. He falls on someone every week. It's harder for him to take when it's me."

"So you've known him your whole life?"

"Most of it. He keeps the game interesting for me," she said with a smile and winced when it hurt.

A hand came down on Todd's shoulder as they continued eating nachos. When he looked up, he shook the hand of the man who had stood next to him.

"Jessie, have you met Officer Phillip Smythe?"

Jessie reached her hand out to shake Phillip's. "No. It's nice to meet you."

"Likewise," Phillip said and shifted his glance back to Todd. "Heard from her?"

"Emailed. She's doing okay."

Phillip let out a breath. "Her mom is home and says she's still working through some other stuff. When you talk to her, tell her we want her home."

"I'll do it," Todd promised.

Phillip settled his eyes on Jessie. "What happened to you?"

"Run-in with Big Finn during a basketball game," she said, and that brought laughter to Phillip's dull mood.

"Least graceful man I've ever met," he humored. "You okay?"

"Yeah, just a little bruised. I'll be fine by next week."

"Well, it was nice to meet you. Todd, I'll talk to you soon."

Phillip went on his way, and they both watched him as he made some patrons look the other way, while others called to him for conversation.

"Who is he worried about?" Jessie asked as she watched Phillip walk out the door.

"Lydia. She's doing some self-recovery, and he's suffering."

"They're an item?"

"In his mind they seem to be. In hers—she can't stand him."

Todd was sure Lydia was about ready to come home, but he'd never give Phillip that impression. When Lydia was ready, she'd face what happened to her, go back to work, and deal with Phillip Smythe on her own terms.

"Are you going to be at the reception hall tomorrow?" Jessie asked as she drank down a glass of water before her next beer arrived.

"I'll be there. Beer order arrives in the morning. I have a guy coming to work on the air conditioner. The carpet cleaners are scheduled to be there in the afternoon. If I'm lucky, Susan will stop by with impromptu lunch again. What about you? You going in to get started on your space?"

The smile that tugged on her lips was hard to keep because of the pain in her nose, but she felt the glory of it. "I'll be there. My parents are very excited for me and my new venture. They wanted to give me money to get started, but I want to do this on my own."

"When do you think you'll be ready to open?"

"I'm shooting for a month."

"Let me know how I can help. I mean, I'm around."

The waitress brought their beers, and she took a long sip from hers. "How are you at painting?"

"Just above pre-school level," he joked. "But I can hold my own."

"I'm picking up paint tomorrow. If you're so inclined, stop by."

With everything he had going on, he wondered just where he was going to find time to help her paint, but he knew he would. He found that spending time with her only made him want to spend more.

Still, he chalked it up to being lonely—and a little desperate. Although he didn't want to come across that way.

They ordered another appetizer—buffalo wings, and a pitcher of water. A baseball game played on the TVs surrounding the bar, and for another hour they enjoyed simple conversation and each other.

The sun was down, stars were out, and the sound of crickets sang to those who would listen as they walked to their cars.

"Get home and get some ice on that bruise," Todd offered as Jessie opened her car door.

"Will do, Doc. Do you have to drive out to the ranch now?"

"I'm at Lydia's while she's gone. So just across town."

She didn't get into her car, he noticed.

"Thanks for coming to the game."

"Wouldn't have missed it for the world."

"Thanks for the drinks and the wings."

"My pleasure. I enjoyed the company."

Those crickets seemed to get louder, he noticed. What else was he supposed to say? For some reason, he didn't want to walk away.

Jessie took a step closer to him. "I'll see you tomorrow."

"I'll be there," he said, feeling like an idiot. He should move in. Kiss her. Hug her. Something other than sounding like an...

Jessie closed the gap, resting her hand on his cheek, she pressed a kiss to his lips and lingered there as if she were waiting for him to notice.

He noticed.

Todd moved in, wrapping his arms around her waist as her arms circled his neck.

Her mouth opened to his, and a wave of warmth flooded through him.

This was what he'd wanted and couldn't gather enough courage to do. Jessie, she was braver than he was, and he knew that.

Her fingers splayed into his hair as her tongue moved against his. The entire world could watch them stand there, and he didn't care.

As she pulled back, she rested her forehead to his. "I'll see you tomorrow."

"Yeah," was all he could say before she turned and climbed into her car. A moment later she drove away, and he stood there watching her disappear.

It had begun, he thought. Now he just had to keep enough nerve to continue. He liked her—really did. But one thing Todd Walker wasn't good at was women.

CHAPTER 11

*J*essie pressed her finger to her burning lip. Between the wings and that kiss, her lip throbbed from the cut that had happened when Big Finn had run into her.

Oh, but it was so worth it, she thought as she rolled down the windows and opened the moon roof.

She was used to making the first move with men. She intimidated them either by her height or her determination.

Todd Walker didn't seem like the kind of man who'd be intimidated by a strong woman. They surrounded him. He did, however, seem like a gentleman who wouldn't take advantage of a woman, and that was noble.

THE NEXT MORNING, Jessie poured her coffee, added ample cream, and sat down at the computer to make a list of things she wanted to accomplish long-term and today. Once satisfied with the list, she printed it out, and made sure it downloaded a copy to her phone and iPad.

After a shower, and some fine makeup skills to hide the

bruises on her face, she headed to the hardware store where a nice man named Earl helped her pick out the perfect color for her reception area and the right shade of white for her studio.

Armed with paintbrushes, paint cans, tape, and tarps, Jessie let herself into the small space ready to begin the adventure she'd set out on when she'd signed the lease.

While parking her car she'd noticed the beer truck out back and the HVAC truck parked next to it. No doubt Todd's day was well underway.

After her second trip into the shop, she looked up to see him standing in the doorway watching her. "You're right on time," she joked as she dropped the bags from her hands. "I'm done."

"My mother always said I had impeccable timing when it came to helping."

For a moment there was an awkward silence between them. It was enough time for Jessie to wonder if she'd made a mistake the night before when she'd kissed him.

But, it only took another moment for him to walk across the room, cup her face, and plant a warm and welcoming kiss on her mouth. "Good morning," he whispered.

"Good morning."

"I've waited twelve hours to do that."

She tried to clear her mind to have a normal conversation, but he really had surprised her with the kiss. "I was afraid I scared you away."

Todd shook his head. "Not going to happen." He took a step back and scanned a look over her. "How's your face?"

"Sore. Lip is very tender."

"Your lip?"

Jessie chuckled as she picked up one of the bags she dropped to the floor and set it on the card table she'd set up. "It got a cut in the shuffle with Big Finn. The wings did a job on it and then when we kissed..." She looked up at him and smiled. "Well, it's sore."

Todd followed her to the table, picking up another bag and setting it next to the one she'd carried over. "Too sore to not kiss for a bit?"

Jessie looked him square in the eyes. "Never too sore for that."

He winked and helped her sort through her items. "Dinner tonight?" he asked as he pulled out paint brushes and tape.

"What did you have in mind?"

Now his head lifted. "Maybe we could eat in. Do you cook?"

"Enough to not starve," she said, folding the empty bag in her hand.

"We're a match made in heaven. That's how I cook. Your place or mine?"

Jessie placed her hands on her hips. "Mine. I don't want to be responsible for burning down Lydia's place with my cooking skills."

That caused Todd to laugh. "I'll bring the groceries. Text me your address."

"Give me your number."

He pulled his phone from his pocket and she added her number, but he remained close. "I have to get back to the hall. I'll come back by and help paint."

"I'll be here."

"That's what I'm finding I like most about all of this. You're right here," he said as he pressed a gentle kiss to her lips before turning and heading out.

THE ONE THING Todd would have to remember was to stay focused on his job at hand now that he and Jessie seemed to be taking their admiration to the next level.

He'd worried over that first kiss of the morning, but now he was invited to her house.

He was gentleman enough to know he'd leave by ten and not stay the night. There was a lot they didn't know about each other, and he wouldn't race right into sleeping together. He wanted to feel this out, and he was damn sure she did too.

The beer driver gave him his invoice, and the HVAC guy came in with a list of things that was needed for the units to keep them running.

This would need to be a call, not just an email to Lydia to confirm all the costs. As he dialed her number, he wondered just how ready she was to coming home. He missed her terribly, but now he didn't want to leave his post.

"Don't be spending my money, Walker," she answered the phone and her voice sounded lighter than normal.

"Why do you think that's the only reason I call you?"

"Because it is." She laughed. "But other than that, how are things going?"

"Can't I just tell you what needs to fixed first?"

He heard the tsk sound through the phone and smiled when she said, "Oh, you're avoiding something personal. What is it? I need gossip."

"Nothing. I just want to wrap all of this up so I can go help the photographer paint her storefront."

"Ah! And she's beautiful, isn't she?"

"Yes."

"Blonde?"

"Yes," he said, knowing he had a weakness for that trait.

"Little bit of a thing? Like Bernadette on Big Bang Theory?" she quoted the title to his favorite TV show, and that made him bust out in laughter.

"Oh, totally the opposite."

"She's a heifer?"

"Lydia!"

Now she was laughing, and that melted his heart to hear it.

"No, she's not. She's a basketball player. She's six-two, beautiful, unique, athletic, smart…"

"And you're sleeping with her."

He shook his head. "No. I'm not sleeping with her. But I'm enjoying her company. So if you'd approve the charges that I need, I can get back to enjoying her company."

Todd gave her the rundown of repairs that needed to be done, and she gave her approval.

"I miss you and all those women you're related to," Lydia said when they'd finished their business.

"And we miss you too."

"And how many times has Phillip been there asking about me?"

He wasn't sure if he wanted to say anything about it, but he owed it to her. "He found me last night when I was out with Jessie. He asked about you. He misses you too."

Todd expected her to get all fired up over it, but she didn't. "I don't think I'll be much longer. I'm working with another therapist here."

"I thought you were done with all of that," he said.

"Your mental health always needs you. I'm giving it what it needs. It doesn't mean I'm manic or anything. It means I'm a healthier version of myself. Maybe you should try it. It'll help you with your daddy issues."

He wanted to argue and tell her he didn't have daddy issues, but they'd been down that road. He did.

They ended their conversation with the words I love you and goodbye. When he hung up the phone, he saw Jessie standing in the doorway.

CHAPTER 12

here had been no need to hear the other side of the conversation to know who he was talking to. Jessie realized at that moment Lydia Morgan was more of a sister to him than just a boss or a friend.

"Everything okay?" she asked.

There was a nervousness in his actions as he closed up his files and stood from behind his desk.

"Yeah. I just had to clear some costs with Lydia."

"That's what I figured." As he rounded the desk, she took a few steps toward him. "You're very kind, Todd Walker. I just want you to know that."

"Why do you say that?"

"Because you had every opportunity to make that phone call crass and unappealing, and yet you made me sound like some kind of freaking Disney princess."

He chuckled. "You were standing there a very long time, weren't you?"

"I need a Starbucks run and I came to see if you wanted something. But yes, I was here for most of it."

Closing the distance between them, he took her hand. "You're more than a Disney princess to me. I think you're all those things I told Lydia you were."

"And you're manly enough to not be in it for sex."

"I'm glad you find that a redeemable trait."

Wrapping her arms around his neck, his came to her waist. "You have no idea how refreshing it was to hear. Especially after I'd invited you to my house."

"I might have been raised by a basket case and an asshole, but I try very hard to uphold the Walker name by being decent."

"No complaints here," she said before she lifted her lips to his and kissed him without regret.

She hadn't planned on sleeping with the man when he came for dinner, and she was strong enough in will and in strength to keep it from happening, but now she wasn't so sure that was what she wanted at all.

How had she happened into a world where he was part of it, and she would get her dream of doing something on her own—in business for herself? Jessie was afraid that she'd wake up to find the entire weekend had been a dream. When she woke, Todd wouldn't know her, she wouldn't be painting the space that was to be her studio. However, that wasn't bothering her as his breath mixed with hers.

When he eased back, he looked at her and she felt the same glorious feeling pass through her as she had when she'd over-heard him speaking about her. "I'll take a grande cappuccino," he said, bringing her thoughts back to why she was standing in his office. "By the time you get back, I'll be done up here and I can come help."

"I won't be long."

She nipped his lips one last time and left feeling just a little light-headed.

.   .   .

THE WALK down to the Starbucks was exactly what she needed. Seeing people tending to their businesses and others shopping and making that happen, she thought about the day she would open her doors to customers.

Before she did that, she would take portraits of her friends and family. Because of Todd, and their generosity, she would extend that complimentary offer to every member of the Walker family as well. She was sure that they would all love to have portraits of their families.

As Jessie opened the door to the coffee shop, Finn nearly fell right out of the door, having moved in to open it with his shoulder. With a coffee in each hand, he only missed ramming into her by a centimeter.

"Oh, hell!" he hollered as coffee spurted through the hole in the lid's top. "Jessie, I swear I don't attack you on purpose."

She laughed. "Where are you going with your hands full?"

"Back to the hardware store. I'm filling in for Dave who threw his back out. His wife and daughter like these fancy coffees, and I wanted to get them each one."

"Can I help you with them?"

Jessie took one cup and walked side-by-side with Big Finn the two blocks to the hardware store.

"How's your face?" he asked.

"It's just fine. Don't you worry about me."

"Oh, I'll always worry about you. How's your sis? Getting her wedding all planned?"

"Yep, it won't be long. I think she and Mom are having a fun time with the planning."

She knew his eyes were on her, so she turned and looked up at him, causing him nearly to trip over the sidewalk.

"Someone told me you were kissing that Walker boy."

Walker boy. She wasn't sure why that humored her, but it did.

"I guess I was kissing that *Walker boy*. So?"

"Nothing. Just know the family. His family. They're different from the other side—you know?"

Big Finn wasn't one to spread rumors, but he was one to worry.

"Todd has told me about his mom and dad. I've seen him around his sister. They are a gracious family."

"No doubt. But his dad…"

"He's not his dad. Besides, it's all new. We're feeling it out. Nothing has happened more than that little kiss someone told you about."

"They didn't say little."

"It didn't feel little, either," she humored as they walked through the door of the hardware store and the conversation about her kissing boys was over.

~*~

TODD HAD LET himself into her studio. She was taking longer than he'd expected, so he figured she wouldn't mind if he got started.

He'd gone straight into taping off the door frame and around the front window, having it nearly done before she walked in with two cups of coffee.

"Oh, I should have taken longer. I was dreading taping off and you have a good start on it," she said as she walked to the folding table and set the cups down.

"I figured I couldn't screw up the tape job."

"Sorry it took so long. Big Finn ran me over again."

Todd hurried off the step stool and moved toward her. "Are you hurt?"

Jessie laughed. "No. He's such a klutz, and I'm safe. He's helping at the hardware store and was juggling multiple cups of coffee. Difficult for him to do that and walk. So I helped him out. Took me a few more minutes."

Todd picked up the cup with the green stopper in it and pulled it out. "You're wrapped around his finger."

Jessie shrugged. "Someone saw us kissing in the parking lot last night. He knew all about it."

"Word travels fast. Was he mad?"

"Inquisitive."

He understood the tone in that. "I'm not Byron Walker."

Jessie sipped her coffee and studied him over the lid. "I said nothing about that."

"I've lived here a long time, and I know if someone is *inquisitive* it means they are comparing me to my father."

She chewed on her lip before she set her cup back on the table and clasped her arms behind her back. "I told him that you had told me about your father, and about your family. If you want some kind of sympathy from me, you're not going to get it. You made it clear to me who you are, and where you're going in your life by your actions. Do you think I give a crap what people worry about? Sure, Big Finn is out to protect me, even if I have a black eye because of him. If I tell him you're a good man, he knows you're a good man."

Todd rubbed his hand over the back of his neck. "I'm sorry. I've put up with it my whole life, and I get a little punchy."

"I'm not judging you. Your paternity doesn't dictate who you are or who you're going to be."

Todd moved to her, closing the space between them. He reached behind her and took her hands, now holding them between them. "Thank you. Sometimes I need to be reminded."

"I'm an honest person. If it bothered me, I'd tell you."

"Thank you. And thank you for the coffee."

"My pleasure. You can pay me back by finishing with the taping. I hate that part."

"We're a good pair then. I can't stand the painting part."

Jessie lifted her arms and laced them around his neck. "Are you good with what's happening here? This new *thing*?"

Todd chuckled. "*Thing*? As in us wanting to kiss all the time?"

"Yeah, that."

"I'm good with it."

"I don't do this. Kiss guys I've just met."

"I don't make a habit of kissing girls I've just met either."

"I don't put up with being one of many."

He understood where she was going with this, and he wondered if she would pull a precisely folded note out of her pocket and ask him to mark yes or no next to the word boyfriend or girlfriend.

"Do I need to reiterate I'm not like my father?"

"Nope, I'm just telling you where I stand."

"If I'm kissing a woman, she's the only one I will be kissing. And you might have heard me tell Lydia I love her, but…"

"She's like a sister."

"Exactly."

"Then I think we're good here."

"I didn't think there was a question."

Jessie pressed a quick kiss to his lips and turned to pick up a paint roller.

Todd took another moment to collect himself. There hadn't been much he'd ever regretted in his life, except for being Byron Walker's son.

CHAPTER 13

*S*tanding in the middle of what would soon be her studio, Jessie nearly wept with delight. She and Todd had worked until dark, painting the walls, and it was beautiful.

"I'm exhausted," Todd said as he walked back in from having washed out the paintbrushes in the parking lot. "Don't tell my mother what we've done. She'll want me to paint every room in her house."

"Do you help your mother a lot?" she had to ask.

He shrugged. "She cons me and Jake into projects once in a while. Usually when her man of the moment flakes out."

It broke her heart that he didn't have great things to say about either of his parents. Jessie couldn't even imagine not absolutely wanting to spend time with her family.

How far could she step over the line and ask questions? Until she did it, she would never know. "Man of the moment? Not married?"

"Not currently," he said nonchalantly as he took a hammer to the lids atop the paint cans. "She's been married numerous times, as has my dad. I have one full brother, and three half-sisters. What more do you want to know?"

"I didn't mean to…"

"You're kissing me, right? It's okay to ask."

She had to laugh at the kissing reference. Was this their cute joke, or were they really avoiding the term 'dating'?

"I am in fact kissing you," she offered the term back to him and he chuckled. "My parents have been married forever. I can't imagine them apart. And that sounded insensitive."

"For those of us not brought up in a family like that, your situation sounds weird." He smiled and moved to her, taking her hands in his. "I'm an open book. But right now, I'm a hungry book. And I'm tired. Are you still up for dinner? Maybe we just grab a pizza and take it home. I won't stay too long."

Jessie contemplated it all—the pizza, the staying. She'd let that play out.

"I think that sounds like a plan. Do you want to call it in? I'll pick up some beers and meet you at my house."

Todd moved his head from side to side, obviously trying to loosen the tension in his neck and shoulders that had landed there after hours of painting. "One more detail. You'll need to give me your address."

~*~

Todd stood in line at the restaurant down the street where he'd called in the pizza order. One of the tables was filled with kids, he figured they were ten or eleven, fresh from soccer practice having a team meal. At the next table were the parents enjoying one another's company over pizza and beer.

Even as a grown man it made him envious to see such a sight. Neither his mother nor father could have been bothered to see them to soccer practice, or any other sport. They'd been so consumed in their own lives, they often forgot they had sons who needed something more.

Todd shook his head at the thought and then focused on the young team again.

Would he have been a good athlete? Could he have gotten a scholarship? Honestly, would he ever get over it?

His mind went back to his conversation with Lydia, and his daddy issues. They extended further than his dad; he had his share of mommy issues too.

That wouldn't make him a desirable catch. Who wanted to put up with a grown man who couldn't even look at a soccer team without getting all worked up?

When he made it to the counter, he recognized the man who was ringing up the orders. Sebastian Grant had been the all-star quarterback of the football team three years before Todd made it to high school. Here he was serving pizzas on a Monday night. He supposed being the best athlete in high school didn't ensure lifelong success.

"Hey, Todd Walker. How the hell are you?" Sebastian reached his hand over the counter and shook Todd's.

"Good. I don't remember seeing you here before."

"New gig." He smiled that flashy Homecoming King smile. "Expecting baby number four. Thought I'd add some cash to the college funds."

"Congratulations."

"Thanks. You married?"

"Me? Nah," he said, and his mind drew right back to Jessie. "Just haven't been lucky enough yet."

"You gotta be the last Walker to get married."

And the statement made his mood plummet. "Last man standing. Someone has to be left to have all the fun."

Sebastian laughed and pulled the pizza from the window that connected to the kitchen. "Looks like you're all set. Tell your brother I said hi. I caught one of his races not too long ago. He's good."

"He sure is. I'll tell him you say hi."

Sebastian gave him an appreciative nod and moved to the next customer.

Carrying the pizza to his car he thought about being the last Walker to marry. It didn't really matter to him. He was happy. He was still doing Lydia a solid favor by working her businesses, and he was enjoying it. When he went back to his life, he'd be out at the ranch and back at his little house down the road from it. The horses would have his attention, and he'd be eating his aunt's fried chicken once a week. His life didn't sound so bad.

Placing the pizza in his passenger seat, he looked down the street toward the *Bridal Mecca*. If he could build something like his sisters and cousins had, what would he build? Jessie was living her dream, and he was there to watch it become a reality. But what did Todd Walker want?

With that on his mind he climbed into his truck and drove toward Jessie's.

~*~

As if a magical bolt of energy had hit her, Jessie zipped through her house stashing anything out of place. Usually her house was tidy, but with everything she'd been doing the past week, things had gotten away from her.

She closed the doors on the laundry closet as she saw the headlights shine through the front window. Just knowing he would walk through the door made her heart race.

Jessie hurried to the door and watched as he sat in the driver's seat for another moment sending a text, she decided. Then he reached for the box and opened his door.

His face lit up when he saw her, and she took that as a very good sign. She didn't do a lot of dating, so she wasn't sure what to expect. The smile on his lips said it was good.

"Fresh pizza." He held up the box on one hand like one of those Italian pizza maker statues and it caused her to laugh.

"Ice cold beer."

"Warm kisses," he offered as he moved in toward her and kissed her gently on the lips.

"I got nothing. That just melted me."

Todd chuckled. "Then we're on the right track."

THE LIVING ROOM WAS SMALL, and right beyond the front door. A covered sofa, a coffee table, and a TV were all that decorated the area.

"I set two beers on the coffee table," she said as she walked toward the kitchen. "We can eat out there. The Knicks are playing."

"Knicks fan?"

She shrugged. "Basketball fan. ESPN is my friend," she joked as she closed the door and took the pizza from him, setting it on the coffee table. "A girl with no agenda can get lost in the squeak of a shoe on a hardwood floor and the sound of a buzzer."

Jessie was grinning as she spoke, but it said a lot, he thought. She was as lonely as he was.

Todd shrugged out of his jacket and laid it on the chair in the corner. "Bathroom? I need to wash my hands."

"Down the hall."

Her decor was plain, no fancy pillows on the couch, no fussy carpets on the floor, no ornate hangings on the wall. Only a few family portraits hung in the hallway, and he assumed she'd taken them.

But when he opened the door to the bathroom, it surprised him. Dainty towels hung on the rack, and delicate scented soaps in the shape of sea shells decorated a plate. There was a small vase with a single flower on the corner of the sink, and she had folded the toilet paper into a neat triangle.

Todd washed his hands, careful not to get water all over. He straightened the towel before he headed back to the living room.

Jessie had served them each a slice of pizza on a plate with small roses on it. Not fine china, but just as pretty.

"Three pointer. All net," she cheered gleefully as she bit into her slice. "I hit the rim every time, but they go in," she boasted, never taking her eyes off the TV.

"I think you and my sister-in-law could hold your own at a sports bar," he humored as he sat down.

"I think women can be well-rounded. Sports and art." She held out her hand and exposed to him her chipped nail polish covered in paint splatters. "Don't think I won't be having a manicure this week to fix this. I'm not all butch."

"I didn't mean it like that."

She shifted her eyes to meet his, and they were soft and kind. "I didn't think you did. I've been razzed about my size and my skills all my life. I'm probably quick to defend my femininity."

Todd reached a hand to her cheek, still traced with the darkness of the bruise that Big Finn had left on her. "You don't have to defend it with me. You're the most beautiful woman I've ever known. And the most desirable one I've ever kissed."

Jessie licked her lips and swallowed hard before she set her slice back on the plate and came at him, in what he'd later consider a pounce, kissing him hard on the mouth.

CHAPTER 14

*T*odd had gone down under her like prey to a wild cat, and that had been Jessie's intention.

She couldn't get enough of kissing him, and though it was moving much too fast, she didn't want to stop at kissing.

His hands moved to her hair, pulling out the band that held it all back in a ponytail. Her hair cascaded down as he pushed his fingers into it while their tongues met in a passionate battle.

Limbs tangled, and breath escaped between them. Todd's fingers trailed from her hair and down her neck. She gasped at the sensitivity of the simple motion and pulled back to look down into his dark, seductive eyes.

"I'm tough, but I'm not easy," she warned and watched his eyes narrow.

"Then get off me and we'll finish dinner," he shot back, his fingers still moving along her throat and collarbone.

"I'm not moving. I just want you to know, this isn't my style. I don't pick up men after meeting them."

"Didn't think you would. Wouldn't hold it against you if you did."

"I don't want you to go home tonight," she admitted, her breath now caught in her lungs.

A smile turned up the corner of Todd's mouth. "Then it sounds like we're having a sleepover. Now, are you going to keep kissing me, or are we going to make a fort and have s'mores?"

Oh, she was going to keep kissing him. The pizza was a lost cause. They would need to warm that up later.

~*~

IN THE DARKNESS OF NIGHT, just past midnight, Todd rolled over and sucked in a breath. A simple, innocent dinner had turned into much more.

Jessie lay next to him gasping for air, but she had a small laugh that would resonate.

"I don't know if I should laugh or cry," she said still taking deep breaths.

He pressed his hand to his chest where his heart raced. "What does that mean?"

"Even when I have done this with men, and never in the first week mind you, I can't recall a time where it took me through the entire house."

A smile formed on Todd's lips. Yeah, they had made a marathon of it. What had started on the couch then led to the kitchen. He recalled that whatever they'd done in the kitchen left them messy, and that had sent them to the shower. From the shower they'd landed in bed where they'd had a few bouts in the bed, on the floor, and in the chair in the corner.

"I don't think you should laugh or cry. Maybe find us an oxygen bottle."

Now she laughed as she rolled to face him.

"It won't make things awkward, will it? I mean, we sort of work together."

Todd took her hand and pressed it to his chest so she, too, could feel the thudding of his heart. "No. I think it only makes working near each other even better. I promise to stay out of your way, but don't hate me if I happen to be admiring from afar." Now he rolled toward her. "Besides. Mine is a temp gig. So I have to enjoy it while it lasts."

Even in the dark, he saw the smile fade from her lips. "I forget that you don't own the building."

Todd chuckled as he lifted her fingers to his lips and pressed a kiss to them. "You'll want to be around Lydia more than you want to be around me. Spitfire and full of that spirit that makes you want to be a better person—that's our Lydia."

"Well, until then, I'll enjoy knowing you'll be walking by the window a few times a day."

She moved in closer to him until her head rested against his chest. A few moments later, Todd could feel her steady breath against his skin. She'd fallen asleep right in his arms, when all along he'd meant to go home after dinner—which they'd left on the coffee table uneaten.

This was the start of something bigger than he could have imagined, he thought as he wrapped his arm around her and pressed a kiss to the top of her head.

The son of Byron Walker would consider that it was time to cut loose, make a change, and run. But Todd didn't want to carry on that legacy. He wanted more, finally. The realization that he was the last Walker of his generation to get married and settle down hit him in the gut.

Was he moving in on Jessie just to remedy that?

Did it bother him that everyone was happily married, and he was only the plus one on an invitation card?

He'd promised himself, and Jessie, that they would only have dinner and he'd head home. In his head, he'd planned that out so they wouldn't end up right where they were. Hadn't he already worried over this, as he did when he entered any relationship with a woman?

And, hadn't it been his worrying over it that had ended every relationship he'd had with a woman?

Jessie rolled away from him, facing the other direction, and he contemplated leaving and heading home until she wiggled back so that her back was now pressed to him. She took his arm and draped it over her.

"You're thinking too hard, Walker. Go to sleep. I'm not ashamed or upset about what happened here. I don't think less of you." Her voice was but a whisper in the dark. "I'm not fragile and neither are you."

He was holding his breath.

She was right. Neither of them would break over this, no matter which way it ended up. And if he didn't start thinking more positively, he could sabotage it, just like he'd done with every other relationship.

But he knew that this woman was different.

He sucked in a breath and pulled Jessie even closer. The woman in his arms was strong enough to take chances and get up off the floor after Big Finn ran her over. She was sincere enough to see the beauty in a portrait and capture it for eternity. And she was secure enough in herself to be wrapped in his arms, by her own doing, and content to sleep. That alone said a lot.

No, Todd Walker, he thought to himself, you're not fragile and you're not your father.

Placing a kiss to Jessie's shoulder, he thrilled at the fact that she moaned at the gentle pleasure. This was the start of something wonderful, and as long as he closed his eyes and fell asleep with her in his arms, he might not talk himself out of it.

CHAPTER 15

*R*ain kept Jessie from washing the outside windows as she'd planned to do. Instead, she was mapping out her display wall.

The portraits she would include on her display walls were scattered throughout the room, propped up against the walls so she could see them.

There were a lot of pictures of her parents and her sister, her sister and her fiancé, and a few family portraits of close friends. She'd done exactly two senior sessions, and a wedding in a field.

What should have been a day to embrace the new start in her life, had only mucked up her confidence. What right did she have to open a business when in fact she hadn't shot more than the people she cared for?

"Wow, this is an impressive collection of pieces," Pearl said as she pushed open the door to Jessie's store. "You do good work."

Standing in front of the portraits, her arms crossed in front of her, Jessie looked back at the pictures and then up at Pearl who was admiring them.

"Interesting," she began, "I was just thinking how I don't know what I'm doing."

Pearl smiled as she picked up a frame that housed the engagement picture of Jessie's sister and her fiancé. "This captures them perfectly. I've been in the wedding business a long time. I can calculate how long a marriage will last by the dress the bride buys and how she handles the people around her." Pearl shifted a smile toward Jessie. "They've got the real thing here, and you captured that. In fifty years, they'll be happy to have this reminder of where they started."

Jessie could feel the tears burn in the back of her throat. "Thank you."

Pearl set the picture down against the wall from where she'd picked it up and chose a smaller portrait that Jessie had taken of Big Finn's great-niece.

"This is sweet. How old is she here?"

"Three weeks. She's just over a year now. We did a cake smash for her first birthday."

Pearl lifted her head, her brows drew together. "A cake smash?"

Jessie chuckled. "Yeah. You do a first-year session, and then you give the baby a small birthday cake and let them have at it. I have friends that are newborn photographers, and they do it all the time. Sometimes you get a well-eaten cake, other times it covers everyone."

"That's fantastic. I wish I had done that."

This, Jessie thought, was a good opportunity to change up the work on the wall. "I would love to photograph your family. I wouldn't charge you. It would be a great way for me to have more pictures on my wall of families that aren't mine."

Pearl set the pictures of Big Finn's niece down and turned to Jessie as she considered the offer.

"I would take you up on that, and I wouldn't mind paying. Your work is good. In fact, maybe we can make a full day of it? Why don't I talk to my sister and cousins? I know they would all love to have a family session."

Jessie swallowed the lump that had formed in her throat. "I would love that."

Pearl tapped a perfectly manicured finger to her chin. "I'll talk to Glenda too. You know what would be fantastic? A full Walker family portrait. Glenda and Everett and their boys and families. And my brothers and sisters and our families."

"You don't want to include your parents?" Jessie asked and then wished she hadn't.

Pearl winced. "We can consider that when we get closer to doing it. My mom and Todd's mom are close friends. I think they commiserate over our father. He, on the other hand, is a piece of work. So we'll consider it."

Jessie's heart ached for them. Todd's description of him wasn't much different and Jessie couldn't even fathom that a man could be so horrible, and his children so bonded.

"I'm going to call Tyson and see what would work best for him. I'll send the other girls over to schedule with you. I think this will be fun," Pearl said as the door opened again and Todd walked through.

"Hey, two of my favorite girls," he mused as he walked toward them. "Sunshine told me to find you," he said to his sister. "Bridezilla is on her way in."

Pearl's shoulders dropped, and she shook her head. It was then he understood why Sunshine, her assistant, sent him with the message. "That marriage will last six months," she informed Jessie. "Kicked her mother-in-law-to-be out of the store during the bridal dress selection. Changed dresses four times. Called me crying over the napkin order, which had nothing to do with her dress, and is coming in today to put it on just one more time. I'm in it for the happily-ever-afters, but once in a while, you have to deal with the ugly stepsisters," she joked as she kissed Todd on the cheek and let herself out of the store.

Todd scanned the room. "This is impressive."

"That's what your sister said, but I have my doubts."

Todd moved to stand behind her and wrap his arms around Jessie. "We're our own worst critics, aren't we?"

"I suppose." She turned, wrapping her arms around his neck. "She wants to do a family portrait with her family, and she will get the rest of your family to do the same. And," she emphasized, "she wants to do a huge Walker family photo shoot with your cousins, aunt and uncle, and all of you."

"I like that."

And like that, she knew, too, that he was fine excluding his father.

"I don't know if I should even put these up," she said looking down at the pictures that lined the wall.

"Let me be your cheerleader. These are all awesome, and can easily be changed out when you produce new ones. That was the point, right?"

She nodded in agreement.

Todd pulled her against him tightly. "Now, I have a meeting in ten minutes. So I came for a power kiss to get me through it. And then, I promise, you won't see me the rest of the day."

"You don't have to stay away."

Smiling down at her, he nipped her nose with a kiss. "No really, I have to go out to the ranch, so you won't see me the rest of the day. But what do you say to dinner?"

"I'd never turn it down."

"Good. Aunt Glenda is making lasagna and told me she'd make me one to take home. Be prepared to be wowed."

Jessie chuckled, so comfortable in his arms. "I'll make a salad and have some wine open."

"That's my girl."

CHAPTER 16

$\mathcal{T}$he drive out to Walker Ranch was peaceful, and since he didn't make it every day, Todd appreciated the quiet.

He found that life in town didn't bother him as much as he'd thought it might, and he'd have to give some consideration to it if things worked out between him and Jessie. Perhaps that was too optimistic to think that far, but he was being hopeful. She'd captured his attention.

Frost-kissed fields flanked both sides of the road. It was funny that since he was making plans, covering for Lydia, months and years in advance, he'd seemed to forget the current. He'd planned weddings for June and July. Holiday parties were being set up now and scheduled for nearly a year out. The meeting he'd had that morning was with the Ladies' Auxiliary. They wanted to rent the reception hall for a craft fair in April. He'd managed it, just as he had every wedding, bar mitzvah, funeral reception, and political rally for the past few months. In fact, after years on the ranch, he found he was actually skilled at organizing things, and he could handle people too. That had been his biggest concern when he'd promised Lydia he'd take care of things in her absence.

When the Walker house came into view, a warmth filled his heart. He wasn't raised in the house, and he'd never lived there, but it was home. As Lydia had pointed out, frequently, he had daddy issues. He supposed it only enhanced them when he drove up to the house, once owned by his grandfather, and remembered how his own father had gambled away the entire ranch. That made his heart ache.

Most of his issues were fueled by jealousy, having not been born to Glenda and Everett Walker. But they'd been there for him his entire life, and his cousins were more like brothers to him. He couldn't really complain. He'd upheld the Walker name, and he was damn proud of it, no matter what side of the lineage it had come from.

As he pulled into the driveway, Everett Walker, his uncle emerged from the house.

Todd hurried out of his truck to take the bag of trash he carried. "I can get that for you."

"I timed this just right," his uncle joked as he happily handed over the bag. "My wife is on a cleaning kick, and I chose today to work from home. I need to remember to pack up that laptop she bought me for Christmas and take it to the barn tomorrow. I could work out of Eric's office, and then I wouldn't be taking out trash."

"I'm sure Eric would love to have you out there."

Todd tossed the bag into the can on the side of the house and then followed his uncle Everett inside.

"What brought you all the way out here?" Everett asked as they walked through the house and back toward the kitchen.

"I was going to meet with Susan. We're going to discuss new catering menus for next fall and Christmas."

He narrowed his eyes on Todd. "We haven't gotten through this winter. Why are you discussing next winter?"

Todd held in the laugh that wanted to escape. For a man who had to think of his animals and crops months in advance, it surprised him that this seemed odd to his uncle. "Always have to be steps ahead when someone comes to book an event."

His aunt pulled off the yellow gloves from her hands at the sink the moment she saw him walk through the door. She was to him in two steps, her hands on his cheeks pulling him down for a noisy kiss.

"I miss you," she said, and it squeezed at his heart. "You get used to having someone around, and then when they're not, a piece of you is missing."

What he wouldn't give to have his own parents say something like that to him.

He smiled at his aunt who was just a bit of a woman. Well into her seventies, anyone would easily mistake her for someone twenty years younger.

"I miss being out here. Lydia's jobs are quite involved, but it's been an interesting challenge, too."

"What do you hear from her? Is she doing okay? I saw her mother in town, but didn't get to talk to her."

"She's healing. I don't think she'll be away much longer, but she wants to make sure she has a grasp on what happened to her. In fact, she mentioned that mental health is important, and we should all make time to take care of ours."

Todd noticed his uncle's discomfort with the subject by the way he turned away and busied himself in the refrigerator. But his aunt continued to nod.

"Lydia is right. It's our mindset that makes us old and keeps us from getting well when we're sick. I'm glad she's getting what she needs. You let her know we miss her, too, when you speak to her next."

"I sure will."

UNABLE TO RESIST his aunt's invitations, he sat and had a sandwich and a cup of tea with her while he filled her in on things going on in town. She'd already heard that he was involved with the photographer, and she approved.

That had set his smile in place as he drove out to his cousin's house, the promised lasagna from his aunt on the seat next to him.

As he drove up in front of the house near the large barn in the center of the Walker property, Susan walked out onto the porch, a baby on her hip.

"Ah, you're just in time for nap time," she humored.

"I could do with a nap," Todd said as he closed the door to his truck and walked up the steps. "Growing like a weed, huh?"

"I can't believe we have two of them. C'mon in. I have some cookies that are cooling and fresh coffee."

Todd followed her into the house which he still marveled at. The old house that had once stood there had burned to the ground. Eric and Bethany narrowly escaped the fire which was set by a deranged obsessed with Bethany's late mother.

When he thought about it, Todd seriously had to credit Lydia with getting her mental health straight. The damage that could be done to others was incredible.

"I'm going to go put her down," Susan said as they walked through the house, stopping at the living room which opened up into the kitchen. "Help yourself to coffee and cookies. There are mugs and plates on the counter."

She disappeared to the back of the house, and Todd heard a door close.

He walked into the kitchen and found that she had dozens of cookies to choose from. Settling on a white chocolate chip and cranberry and a chocolate chip cookie, he poured a cup of coffee and carried his loot to the counter. Sitting in one of the high-backed stools, he set his items in front of him, and started in on them.

One thing was for sure, he'd eaten better when he worked on the ranch.

Todd had helped himself to more cookies before Susan returned.

"Can I get you a cookie?" she asked, and he chuckled.

"I've had enough of them for now," he admitted.

"I'll send you home with a box." She moved to the coffeepot and poured herself a cup. "So, tell me about this woman you're seeing."

Todd stopped lifting his mug toward lips and looked at her over the top of it. "News travels fast."

"I knew when I met her at the bridal shop that she would be important to you. Tell me all about her."

CHAPTER 17

*J*essie had tossed a salad and opened a bottle of wine, just as she'd promised. She'd lit a few candles and preheated the oven to warm the lasagna. Now she waited for a man, which she'd never done before. What kind of seriousness was this, she wondered.

With a glass of wine in her hand, Jessie sat down on the couch and turned on the basketball game. The Lakers versus the Warriors, that was a game worth watching.

Only a few minutes into the first quarter, Jessie saw Todd's truck pull up in front of her house. Warmth spread though her body just knowing he had arrived.

Jessie walked to the kitchen and poured him a glass of wine. Before Todd could ring the doorbell, she opened the door and saw the warmth that flashed in his eyes.

"What a sight," he said as he stepped onto the porch. "A beautiful woman and a glass of wine."

"I was thinking the same thing. A man and a lasagna," she joked as she handed him the glass of wine and took the wrapped pan from him. "I have the oven on to warm this."

Todd followed her into the house, stopping briefly by the TV. "What game is this?"

"Lakers and Warriors."

"I've never dated a woman who voluntarily had on sports," he said as he walked toward the kitchen where Jessie slid the pan into the oven. "Glenda says it'll only need twenty minutes."

Jessie nodded and set the timer. "Then that gives us a few minutes."

Turning to Todd, she took his glass and set it on the counter. Then she wrapped her arms around his neck and took his mouth with hers. She'd been dreaming of kissing him like that all day, and now she eagerly fulfilled that need.

TODD WRAPPED his arms around Jessie's waist, taking in the sweetness she offered. Oh, how easily he could accept this as normal now. He'd been standoffish about his brother, sisters, and cousins all rushing off and getting married, but in her arms, he could see the charm in having someone to go home to every day.

"This is the best way to end a day," he said when their lips had parted, but their arms remained around one another.

"It is. Maybe after dinner we can discuss you staying the night. It was a good way to start the day too."

Todd brushed a strand of hair from her forehead and lingered his hand on her cheek. "I packed a little bag just in case. I rather enjoyed that kind of start to my day too."

A warm smile crossed Jessie's lips as she turned to pick up his wine. Handing it to him, she took his hand and led him to the living room, where her wine waited and so did the game.

"How was your visit with your aunt and Susan?" she asked as she sat down and lifted her glass to her lips.

"Nice. Glenda sat me down for sandwiches," he said with a chuckle. "She likes to feed people and gather information, though you don't realize that's what she's doing when you're spilling your guts."

"I have a grandmother like that."

"By the time I got to Susan's, she seemed to know all about you. I'm not sure if that was a phone call from Glenda during the time I was driving to Susan's, or if my sisters have already put two and two together."

"You did say I was one of your favorite girls this morning when you walked into my shop while your sister was there."

"I did do that." He sipped his wine. "And Pearl knows relationships. She makes a living on them."

Jessie turned toward him. "Is she usually right? I mean about being able to tell how long a marriage will last?"

"Usually she can call it within months. It's a strange skill."

Easing back against the couch, she smiled. "Then my sister will be happy for a long time."

"And that makes you happy?"

"Of course. I only want what's best for her. She deserves to be happy. We all do."

"And you come from a happy home, don't you?"

Jessie tilted her head and considered the question. "I do. We had some serious down times when Freddie died. Mom and Dad almost didn't make it through that—their marriage I mean." She sipped her wine. "Dad refused counseling, but Mom got it. Dad drank more. Mom prayed more. Carlie and I dove into school activities. I played more basketball. But we managed, so yes, I came from a happy home. What about your brother and sisters? What was Pearl's call on their marriages?"

"They'll all be married forever." He chuckled when he said it. "I have to admit, I'd been skeptical with Audrey because she married a famous and sexy actor. But he dotes on her. Jake, he has his hands full with matched wit from Missy, but it works. Pearl knew what she wanted when it showed up. And the fact that she married a Morgan makes her all the more a badass. But I think that knowing Bethany is in a solid and loving marriage forever, that makes me happiest," he admitted. "She had a rough start. Hell, she had it rough until she came here. She lost her mother to drugs and did her own time in rehab. She has a solid foundation to raise her family now. She's happy and healthy and in love with a wonderful man."

"What more could you ask for, right?"

He nodded. "I can smell that lasagna now. Man, that brings back memories."

"Good ones?"

He shrugged. "Yes. Good ones because Aunt Glenda always doted on us, me and Jake that is. She'd make that lasagna for Christmas every year when we were forced to spend the day with my dad. But then all of their boys would be around, and my grandfather would sit in his chair and fall asleep after Christmas dinner and make weird noises." He chuckled. "Who knew the smell of lasagna could take you down memory lane like that?"

"My great-grandmother would make caramel corn for Christmas dessert. So you'd be stuffed from all the food you ate, and then she'd be in the kitchen making popcorn. I can't go by one of those stores in the mall without buying a bag. It's never ever as good, but even thinking about it makes my mouth water."

"All of this talk just makes me realize I'm lacking in any kind of talent that my non-existent kids will find amazing."

Jessie leaned her head on his shoulder. "I know of a few talents you have, but those aren't the kind you discuss with kids."

He felt the heat rise in his cheeks at that. "I'll find something to impress them." Setting down his glass, he took hers and did the same. "But, since you brought it up, maybe I could impress you with those skills before dinner."

It was Jessie who stood first and headed toward the hallway to the bedroom. As she walked away, she pulled her sweatshirt over her head and let it drop as she kept on walking.

CHAPTER 18

*J*essie worried that she'd already gotten too used to Todd waking in her bed, showering in her bathroom, and making her coffee before he headed to work. Every night they'd plan dinner, and he'd say he would head home. And every night Jessie asked him to stay.

What would happen when Lydia came back and he went back to his regular life, she wondered over the coffee he'd made for her before leaving with a kiss?

He'd promised that Sundays were normally easy, and he'd be back in an hour. But it was his job to open the reception hall for the community church that used the facility on Sunday mornings. Lydia's brother Tyson would close up when services and functions were over later in the afternoon.

Jessie took the time to sit on her couch and watch the Sunday morning news, just as she had every Sunday since she'd lived on her own. Sundays were for cleaning house, taking walks with her camera, and ending with a game at the Y, followed by beer with the guys.

She pressed her hand to her cheek, the trace of Big Finn's

blunder long gone. Would Todd worry about her tonight, in a normal game where anything was possible?

Wrapping her hands around her mug, she smiled to herself. She had a man in her life that would worry. This wasn't something she saw coming when her sister said she was getting married. In fact, when her sister had announced her engagement, she'd gone through a little depression. Relationships hadn't been important to her, and she hadn't had the time to put into one. But now she was in one. A man nearly living in her house constituted a relationship.

A smile formed on her lips. She was in a relationship with Todd Walker. Her heart fluttered in her chest at the very thought of him. What a glorious feeling it was.

~*~

Todd watched the parishioners of the church file into the reception hall. He'd often stayed in his office while their services were held. Today, he would complete a few tasks, send a few emails, and then sneak out the side door and head back to Jessie.

As he checked his alcohol inventory, his cellphone rang, and she smiled as he lifted it to his ear.

"You knew I was sitting in your office, didn't you?" he asked and Lydia laughed on the other end.

"It's Sunday morning. Church is in session."

"It's like printing money, isn't it? Between the church paying to be here weekly, I've booked three more organizations that use the facility bi-weekly. I set up a few tables and collect the check at the end."

"Oh, you're becoming a heartless money monger."

"Your money," he reminded her. "I just want what you built to be here when you come home."

"And I think I'll be home soon," she said, and Todd sat up straighter in his chair.

"Really? You're ready?"

"One can only take the serenity of Hawaii so long," she chuckled on the other end of the phone. "But seriously, I miss my life, and I have a plethora of new tools to use to balance myself. I've dealt with some serious emotional issues, and I will be a better person for it. Now if something bad comes my way, I can deal with it."

Todd thought nothing as bad as what she went through would happen to her again. Whether or not she liked it, he was sure he wasn't the only one who wouldn't let her out of their sight again.

"I can't wait for you to get back," he admitted, and he heard the sigh on the other end.

"I want to get back before you run off and marry that new girl of yours." Her tone had become playful.

"I don't think that'll happen. But I have been staying with her all week. I won't lie, it's nice to wake up in someone's arms that you care about."

"I don't remember, but I'm sure you're right."

He knew it was meant sincerely, but he felt the hurt in her voice. "When are you thinking you'll be home?"

"In a month or so. I have some things to wrap up here. I couldn't just do therapy twenty-four seven. I had to stir up some business too."

Now he laughed a hearty laugh. "Oh, you are a business-minded kind of woman, aren't you?"

"You know it."

"I miss you. We all miss you."

"I miss you all too. Even those of you who don't leave me alone."

That spoke volumes, he thought, but he wouldn't mention anyone by name.

"Okay, Walker. Go collect more checks and make me some money."

"I'm on it, boss. I love ya. Take care of you."

"And I love you. I love all of you. Pass that on."

"Will do," he agreed, and they said their goodbyes. As he shoved his phone back into his pocket, there was a knock on the office door. Hopefully, his phone call hadn't been too loud.

He walked around the desk and pulled open the door to see Phillip Smythe standing there.

"Got a sec?" he asked, and Todd stepped back to let him in.

"What's up?"

Phillip fussed with the hat he held between his hands, this time a baseball cap, and not from his uniform.

"We've had a few break-ins up and down the street the past few nights. They're not taking much, but they're busting through back doors and small windows."

"I hadn't heard about it."

"Like I said, they're not taking much. So it's low key. Just wondered if you'd had any problems."

Todd shook his head. "I would have called it in."

"Figured you might. You have cameras on the parking lot, right?"

"I do. Do you need the footage?"

"Would appreciate anything you have."

Todd moved to the desk and wrote himself a note. "You know Lydia monitors everything."

"Yeah, she's thorough that way."

"I'll send it on over to you," Todd promised.

"Thanks." Phillip turned to the door and then back again. "Talk to her lately?"

"Just got off the phone with her."

The slightest smile formed on Phillip's lips. "She's doing okay?"

"She said she's about ready to come home."

The smile widened. "That's good to hear. Thanks again."

Phillip let himself out of the office, closing the door behind him.

Todd eased into the chair behind the desk and brought up the cameras. He watched as Phillip left the building and walked toward his beat-up pickup truck and climbed in. He didn't drive away. Instead, he sat there for a moment, and Todd couldn't make out what he was doing. Taking a moment, he supposed. Lydia being gone had taken its toll on all of them—especially Phillip Smythe.

CHAPTER 19

*B*ethany fixed her daughter's dress as she positioned her in the small chair, just as Jessie had instructed. The little girl was fidgety, but that was normal for a toddler.

Jessie made a note to add more toys to the box she'd planned to have in the studio. Over the past two weeks, she had photographed every young Walker. This was the last, and she'd never say it aloud, the most precious.

Abigail Walker had a cherub face and Shirley Temple curls and was the spitting image of her mother.

"Sit very still," Bethany instructed her daughter as she backed away from the chair.

Abigail's eyes went wide and then Jessie distracted her with a funny squeaky toy. When she laughed, Jessie knew she'd captured the most perfect portrait of the child.

She heard the front door open, but she didn't move from her perch. Abigail was just warming up, and Jessie was sure that the movie star in her was about to bust loose—after all, she was the daughter of a former movie star. It was to be expected.

"Hey," Bethany whispered as the person who had walked through the door walked into the studio. Jessie didn't have to turn to know it was Todd. She could sense him now, and it warmed her from head to toe.

However, when Abigail saw her uncle, the session was over as she bound from the little chair and straight for his arms.

"There's my big girl," he said, picking her up and planting a noisy kiss on her cheek.

"I think you just ruined her session," Bethany said, but Jessie turned the camera on them, and kept snapping.

The littlest Walker babbled to her uncle, and he hung on every note of her voice. He'd nod his head and agree to anything she mumbled as she played with the button on his shirt, or the pen behind his ear.

These were the moments worth capturing, Jessie thought.

She wasn't oblivious to what seeing him coo over the little girl was doing to her insides. Sexy wasn't a shirtless man on the cover of some magazine. No, it was a man holding a child he adored.

They finished the session, with Uncle Todd in the background, and that seemed to bring out an extra sparkle in Abigail's eyes. She, too, was obviously as taken by the man as Jessie was.

When they finished, Bethany packed up her daughter, and they both hugged Jessie and Todd before heading out the door.

"I didn't mean to hijack your session," he admitted as he pulled Jessie to him and kissed her gently on the lips. "This was all I was coming for."

"She's enamored with you," Jessie said as she lifted her arms to drape around his neck. "I think they both are. It's nice to see a family that's so close."

"You're close with yours."

"Yes, and that's a rare thing."

"As dysfunctional as my family is, you're right, all of us are close. We have each other's backs."

"It shows." Jessie looked around the room. "I just have to clean up props and then I'm done here."

"I have one more meeting," he said with a sigh as he ran a

hand up Jessie's back. "What do you say to a quiet evening at home?"

"I say that sounds nice."

"And what do you say to having that quiet evening at my home? The one out by the ranch?"

Jessie eased back to take him in. "Your house? I'll admit, I forgot you had that house."

Todd chuckled as he lifted his hand to her hair and tucked a loose strand behind her ear. "I forget it too. I haven't checked up on it in a while. Besides, a night under stars that aren't clouded over by city lights is what my soul could use right now."

"I'm looking forward to it."

"You finish up and go home. I'll meet you at your place and then we'll head out."

Jessie nodded and nipped his lips with one more kiss. "I'll grab some groceries. I'm thinking anything you have there won't be something I'll want to eat."

TODD FINISHED HIS MEETING, which landed him another wedding reception for the hall, and an appointment with Pearl for a dress selection. Phillip had called and asked for more footage of the parking lot, hoping to catch a car that might have driven by after they broke into another store.

The drive to Jessie's had become as normal to him as breathing. He found that he enjoyed every moment with her. Were they just having fun, or was this going to turn into something serious?

When he thought about it, it was serious. In the month they'd been together, they'd lived together, worked together, and had most meals together.

Last week she'd taken him home to have dinner with her parents, which he thought had gone well. And Glenda had invited them for lunch the following Sunday.

As he pulled up to Jessie's house, he laughed at the thoughts that had been occupying him on his drive about being 'Todd plus one' when invited to dinners and functions—forever. Forever was a long time to plan for when he'd only been with Jessie for a month.

He noticed her walk by the window, and his heart rate kicked up. Did love really have a time frame? Any hesitation on his behalf was him projecting his father's life on his own. In his heart, he knew that he loved Jessie and when the moment was right, he'd tell her. But he wanted that moment to be special.

She stopped by the window and looked out to him sitting in his truck. With a quizzical look, she waved.

Todd waved back and climbed from his truck. Yeah, he thought, he'd make the moment special when he told her how he felt. But he wouldn't wait much longer.

CHAPTER 20

Todd's truck bounced down the familiar dirt road toward the ranch where he would veer left to head home instead of right which would take him to the ranch.

As he made the turn, his little house came into view. Compared to the newer home that Jessie lived in in the city, his looked as if it had been built a century ago and forgotten. It was funny what nearly nine months away from his house would do to it.

He hadn't neglected it completely. Before he'd met Jessie, he'd stay the weekends at his house and do the things that needed tending to. But once Jessie had come into his life, the little old farmhouse didn't seem so important.

"It has character," Jessie said as she raised the camera she kept on her lap and snapped a picture.

"That it does."

"I mean it." She snapped again. "I think I'll miss the sun behind the house, but maybe tomorrow night I can capture it. And the sunrise."

Todd shifted a glance her way and saw her face light up at the thought of getting that perfect shot—that masterpiece.

"You can take pictures of it from every angle, any time of the day. You're always welcome here."

She smiled from behind the camera. "Thank you." She lowered her camera as he pulled up next to the house. "People are the most interesting subjects, but nature and old houses..." she paused and drew in a breath. "They're mesmerizing."

He hadn't thought about it before, but she was right. Until he'd watched her joy of just seeing the old house, it had just been an old house to him. Sure, it was home, but it wasn't as special as she'd made it out to be.

THEY CARRIED in the groceries and the bag of clothes they'd packed. Todd went straight to the fireplace to light a fire, and Jessie headed to the kitchen.

"When I open this refrigerator, is anything going to jump out at me?"

Todd chuckled from the other room. "I can't promise you that."

She blew out a breath and slowly opened the door. A rush of relief washed through her when she saw that it was nearly empty, clean, and only condiments lined the shelves on the door.

"How often do you come out here?" she asked.

"I was coming out every weekend." Jessie heard him walk across the floor and a moment later was standing in the doorway. "Is it bad?"

"No. Clean and empty."

Todd pushed his shoulders back and smiled, obviously proud of himself. "You've only been with me as a guest in your house, but I'm a neat and tidy guy."

Jessie knew that about him just from the interior of his truck. "I feel bad you haven't been out here in a month."

Todd shrugged. "Why feel bad?"

"You're spending all your time with me. You took over for

Lydia and now you don't come back home because of me. Don't you feel as if we have uprooted your life?"

He moved to her, and she stood to meet him.

Todd wrapped his arms around her waist and pulled her in. "I chose both things. I want to be there for Lydia, and I kind of dread the day that it's not part of my life. And I choose to be with you, every moment of the day. I'm surprised you haven't grown tired of me yet."

"I don't think that'll happen," her voice was soft as it carried her truth.

"I'm glad, because I've been doing a lot of thinking about us."

Her breath caught in her lungs, but she managed to appear calm. "What things are you thinking?"

He brushed his fingers through her hair and rested his hand on her cheek. "Maybe we could think about living together, not just staying with each other."

Jessie steadied her hands on his shoulders because she had suddenly gone dizzy. "You want to live with me?"

"I want to live together. It can be at your place, or maybe we can find our own place. Something that's just ours."

Jessie stepped back and paced the small space. "That's a lot to think about."

"Then maybe this isn't the right time to tell you I love you?"

She turned to him and stared. "Oh, God. You love me?"

Todd stepped toward her but stopped short of reaching her. "Listen, I get it if you don't feel the same about me. I just thought…"

"I love you, too," she blurted to stop him from saying anything more. "I thought I was crazy, since it's been a month, but I love you."

A smile formed on Todd's lips as he closed the gap between them, pulling her into him. "Okay then. We've gotten over that big hurdle. What do you think about us living together?"

Jessie swallowed hard. "It scares me as much as you telling me you love me."

"You realize we've been living together?"

She chuckled, resting her hands on his chest. "You're right. And you should have equally as much space in a home as I have then. My lease has four more months. Maybe we can look for something, together."

"I'd like that."

Jessie pressed her cheek to his. "I would too."

As they sat in the living room that night, wrapped in a quilt his grandmother had made him, a fire roaring in the hearth, they made plans to live together. Todd had decided to lease out his house, and it would be extra income. He felt better about having some options to help with their lease payment since he wasn't sure how much longer his employment would last. The other thing he needed to consider was whether he'd return to the ranch when Lydia returned.

In any big city, he'd drive forty-five minutes to work and back. That was the average time on a freeway. At least his job, which still awaited him, was on a peaceful dirt road to the ranch his grandparents built.

He supposed there would be time to consider his career path. No need to worry about it while he was warm and safe in his home with the woman he loved in his arms.

CHAPTER 21

*J*essie scanned over her schedule for the day. She had a consultation with a bride which Pearl had sent over, to do an engagement session. At two, she had a newborn session, also referred by Pearl, who had been instrumental in the wedding dress decision for the mother two years earlier.

Lifting her head, Jessie gazed out the front window of her store as Ellie passed by on her way to her office and waved. She was part of the Walker women—those born a Walker, and those who had married in.

The very thought had her heart thumping harder. She was about to embark on living with a Walker man, so was she considered a Walker woman too?

She realized she'd pushed her shoulders back and lifted her chin. Walker women had a confidence that she could only wish for. They were proud, strong, and so smart. And, she reminded herself; she worked among them. They sent their business. They fed her lunch. They'd invited her out for drinks after work.

Yes, she was becoming a Walker woman, and she hadn't even known she wanted to be one.

The chime above the door pulled her from her thoughts.

Phillip Smythe walked through the door, pulling off his hat, and holding it between his hands.

"Ms. Hanson," he said with a nod in her direction.

"Officer Smythe. It's nice to see you. How can I help you?"

"We've been having some break-ins of businesses up and down the street over the past month."

"Todd mentioned that."

"Well, last night they kicked in Gia's back door."

Jessie's teeth clenched. Her store was right next to Gia's gift shop filled with Italian treasures. "Did they take anything?"

Phillip shook his head. "No. They must have been scared away by something. They got the door kicked in, but then ran. Todd just shared the video footage with me."

"That's horrible."

"I know you're all tight here, I just want to make sure you all are safe. If you notice anything—anything at all, call me. If you feel unsafe, call 9-1-1."

"Of course."

The door opened again and Todd walked through.

"Gia and Dane are next door if you want to talk to her," he said to Phillip. "Dane has her calm now. He'll stay with her today."

"That's a good idea. I'll talk to Ellie before I take off." He shifted a glance back to Jessie. "Again, don't hesitate to call."

"I will. Thank you."

Phillip nodded toward her again as he slipped back on his hat and walked out of her store.

Jessie looked at Todd. "Is Gia okay?"

"She's shaken up."

"She should be. That's so scary."

Todd rubbed his fingers over his chin. "I can't tell if they're teenagers or just scrawny men trying to break in. They wear dark hoodies, and the minute her door opened, they ran the other way."

"You didn't see their faces?"

"No. They wear their hoods up and bandanas over their nose and mouths. They hit the barbershop across the street a few days ago, and the pizza shop last week."

Jessie could feel her palms grow damp, and she wiped them on her pant leg. "Okay, now I'm a little freaked out."

Todd moved to her and pulled her to him. "Don't be. They're not coming in during business hours, and I'm always here. In fact, if they know what's good for them, they stay away altogether, because I wouldn't want to cross the women of the *Bridal Mecca*. I fear for myself often."

Jessie laughed and rested her head on his shoulder.

"They all invited me out for a drink after work today."

Todd kissed the top of her head. "Ah, you've been accepted into the tribe."

"I like that."

"So do I." He kissed her again and stepped back. "Beer truck just pulled up. I can hear his brakes. I'll grab some subs for lunch and bring them before your first session."

He blew her a kiss and hurried back to his work, and she decided she needed to get back to hers. She wanted to get Bethany's proofs to her before they went for drinks.

Looking back at the front door, and then toward her workstation in the back of her studio, she decided to lock the door. She'd set an alarm on her phone to unlock the door for her client, and Todd had a key. But at the moment she was feeling a little uneasy about the door being open and anyone walking in.

~*~

. . .

TODD STUDIED the footage again of the two men kicking in Gia's door. She was the only one with valuables in her store, he decided, and that must have been why they hit her first. But why hadn't they taken anything?

He rewound the images trying to see something he'd missed the first fifty times he'd watched it.

What could they do to protect the stores better?

Bethany strolled into the office and sat down in one of the chairs that faced him. "Why does this happen on our watch and did anyone tell Lydia?"

"Why tell her? She can't do anything about it." He stopped and froze the image that exposed the men the most, yet was still unwilling to give them any clue to who the men were. "Phillip is on this, and it's not just focused on the *Bridal Mecca*. It's all over town."

Bethany pulled a piece of lint from her skirt. "I just hope they find them before they cause serious damage to someone's store."

Todd agreed. "Dane is still with her?"

"Yeah, he'll be here all week he said. She's really shook up."

"I know. Jessie has her door locked and Ellie took her laptop home to do some work. Pearl has on every sharp sample ring in her jewelry case so that if they do come in, she can punch them and do maximum damage."

That drew a laugh from his sister. "Audrey wonders if they've been into her salon too. But then she always gets the crazy ones in there."

"Phillip has had a car driving by every half hour. Everything will be fine."

Bethany leaned in toward the desk and pulled back a flyer he'd been looking at. "Two bedroom, two bath, two-car garage." She lifted her eyes to him. "Two miles from here with a small yard and walking distance to the open space. Moving to the city? Lydia coming home?"

Todd eased back in his chair. "Lydia will come home, and she'll want her house back."

"But you have a house," she reminded him.

"I do and I'm going to lease it out."

"And live in town?"

"With Jessie."

Her eyes went wide. "This is more serious than I thought. Shacking up with the photographer."

Todd chuckled. "I like her. I like her enough to have told her I love her."

Bethany pressed her fingers to her lips. "You're in love."

"If you cry you have to leave."

"I'm happy for you." She set the flyer back on his desk. "Pearl's going to start planning your wedding, you know."

"And I haven't discussed this with Pearl, so..."

"Right." She held up a hand. "She won't find out tonight over drinks either."

"You're all still going for drinks?"

Bethany stood and headed toward the door. "After today we all need one, and we have to plan you know. Walker women are prepared for people breaking into our stores and for weddings for our brothers." She smiled widely.

"We're not getting married."

As Bethany walked out of the office, she hummed letting him know that the secret of him moving in with Jessie would no longer be a secret. Perhaps he should tell Jessie before his sisters, sister-in-law, and wives of his cousins began to wear her down for more information.

Todd hit play on the video one more time and then turned off the computer. Maybe he'd just let them all talk and see what kind of mood Jessie was in when she came home. He could judge from that whether marriage was something on her mind.

CHAPTER 22

*B*ecause it had been on her mind all day, when Jessie locked up her studio for the night, she piled chairs and props at the back door to ensure anyone who kicked in the door would have a nasty fall if they gained access.

When she felt that she'd created a sufficient barrier, she locked the front door and headed to Pearl's.

The sign said closed, but she could see the back lights on and Sunshine waved her inside.

"They're gathering in the back," she said as Jessie walked through the door.

"Are you going with us?"

Sunshine shook her head. "My little peanut has a fever and is calling for mama. Her daddy is totally capable of taking care of her, but it just warms my heart that she wants me."

"That is precious. I hope she feels better soon."

"Nothing some juice, some hugs, and a good Disney movie can't fix. Let Pearl know I'm locking the front door on my way out."

"I will," Jessie agreed and walked back to the area Pearl used to showcase the brides trying on dresses.

Missy stood up on the small stage between the three full-length mirrors and checked her outfit from every angle. Bethany stood behind her pulling on the back of Missy's blouse.

"I think it's time you bought a maternity shirt," Bethany said. "This won't fit much longer."

"I hate buying clothes. Why do I want to buy something I only get to wear for a few months?"

"Because at least it'll cover your ass," Pearl said as she walked out from the back room. "Jessie!" she shouted, and all eyes turned to her standing in the doorway. "Missy will need a maternity shoot. When do you do that? Eighth month?"

"Ideally," Jessie agreed. "Congratulations."

"Can't race cars with a pregnant belly," Missy moaned. "Eh, time files anyway, right?"

Jessie wasn't sure Missy was happy about the baby, but the rest of the room was. Then again, Missy had a hard exterior, as she would assume any female race car driver would. Deep down she was probably fine with being pregnant.

"We thought we'd head over to Mick's for drinks. Does that sound okay?"

Jessie nodded. "Of course. They have my favorite beer on tap."

"We can all leave our cars here and walk over," Pearl said as she picked up her purse from the chair next to her and pulled it up to her shoulder. "Gia is already over there. Dane took her for an early dinner."

"Is she doing okay?"

Audrey stood from her seat on the couch. "She's shaken up, but Dane fixed the door to her shop. He reinforced the frame and the lock. They added a bar. It's all good. Tomorrow she'll be right as rain."

"I kept my door locked most of the day too," Jessie admitted. "Just felt safer."

Pearl swept her hand through the air as if to wipe away the conversation. "Let's not talk about this the rest of the night. We have better things to dish about," she announced as they all walked out of the store and Pearl locked the door behind her. "Jessie, Bethany says you and Todd are looking for a place."

Jessie felt the shock of the statement hit her right in the chest. They hadn't discussed that with anyone. Well, she hadn't, anyway.

"We're looking at getting our own place, yes," she admitted, because what good would it do to deny it?

Bethany moved in beside her and linked their arms together. "To save Todd some face, he didn't tell me. I saw the flyer, and I annoyed him until I got my answers. It's a big step," she said as they crossed the street toward the pub on the corner. "Things are going well between the two of you?"

Pearl opened the door to the pub, and the noise filtered into the street. "Talk at the table. I don't want to miss out on anything," she stated with a well-manicured finger in the air. "I mean it."

Bethany kept her arm linked with Jessie's as they walked to the back corner of the pub and inhabited a large corner booth. Gia joined them, and Ellie joined a few minutes later.

When they were all situated, and they had ordered their drinks, Pearl turned her attention to Jessie. "Okay, now tell us all the details about you and Todd."

All eyes were on her and she could feel the heat rise around her. "Well, he's been mostly living at my house, anyway. We decided that maybe it would be something to consider—us living together that is."

Pearl nodded thoughtfully. "That's all? Just shacking up?"

"That's all."

"You love him?"

Jessie swallowed hard. These were her friends, and as close to co-workers as she had. But it was Todd's sister that was shooting the questions at her. Did he want his family to know all of this?

He was the one who had somehow told Bethany. It wasn't really a secret.

"Yes," she finally said. "I love him. We've exchanged words. We've been practically living together since we met, and now we're going to get a place that's just ours. He's going to lease his place. Lydia will come back soon, and we want something we both are part of, not just him moving into my space."

Jessie realized she'd rattled that all off without taking a breath.

Gia lifted her glass. "To new beginnings for the last Walker man to be claimed."

"Cheers," they all said in unison and they raised their glasses.

From then on, the conversation moved around the table. The women talked about kids and businesses. Each of them had something gracious to say about Todd's aunt, who was not present. They talked about a spring picnic out at Susan and Eric's in May, and when the conversation came back to Jessie, they asked her about basketball on Sundays.

She was part of this clan more than she'd realized, and she wanted to be a full member of their little club. She chuckled as she raised her beer to her lips. Loving Todd Walker had its perks.

CHAPTER 23

$\mathcal{T}$odd heard Jessie's car pull into the driveway. He muted the TV and waited for her to walk through the door.

"You must have had a nice time," he said as she came into view.

"I did," Jessie agreed as she dropped her purse in the floor and moved to sit next to him on the couch. "You're going to be an uncle again. Did you know?"

He grinned. "I did know. She wasn't ready to say anything yet. I guess she mentioned it?"

Jessie shrugged. "I don't know if she mentioned it or if Bethany just outed her."

He chuckled. "Bethany has skill with that."

"She let everyone know we were moving in together, too."

He flinched at that. "She saw the flyer. Sorry about that."

Jessie took his hand and held it in hers, intertwining their fingers. "I told them that we'd decided to move in together, and that we'd told each other we loved each other."

"Wow. You're in tight with my sisters now, huh?"

She rested her head to his shoulder. "I like it. I feel like I belong with them. Does that make sense?"

Todd kissed the top of her head. "It totally makes sense. You're just like all of them. Kind. Compassionate. Entrepreneurial. And hooked up with an amazing guy."

Jessie lifted her head and pressed a kiss to his lips. "I am hooked up with an amazing guy. But don't be surprised if your sister wants to start measuring you for tuxedos. You are, after all, the last of the Walkers to walk down the aisle."

She was joking about it, he thought. Was this what she wanted?

"I am. What do you think about that? About my sister wanting to marry me off?"

She noticed his beer on the coffee table, reached for it, and took a sip. "I think if we decided that living together was the right thing, then the next step would be to marry the last of the Walker men. But I also think both of us believe that this needs just a little more time before we make that decision."

"Then we'll follow up on this conversation after we move in together."

She took another sip of his beer and then handed it to him. "I'd like that. For now, I'm going to go take a hot shower and go to bed." She stood and looked down at him. "I have a place on my back that I just can't reach." She lifted her brows.

Todd finished his beer and discarded the empty bottle back to the coffee table as she stood. "I can help with that."

"I was hoping you might."

~*~

SITTING AT HIS DESK, filling out purchase orders the next morning, Todd realized he wore a permanent grin on his face. All night he'd been thinking about being the last of the Walker men to take the vows. Seriously, he hadn't expected to be giddy about the prospect of closing that gap. But when he thought of his brother, his sisters, and his cousins, they were all happy. They were all living their dreams, had someone to share that with, and now they had children. His Christmas shopping list had doubled in size, and he was happy about that.

Jessie had had a photo shoot first thing that morning, and as she talked to her client, Todd had sat at her workstation having a cup of coffee. Listening to her describe what they'd be doing and what images she was hoping to capture made his heart swell. Having that much joy for someone else's success could only mean that the love he felt for her was true and pure. Why shouldn't he marry her?

As he sat there, an email chimed on his computer and pulled him from his thoughts. It was from his mother, and suddenly the thoughts of happy marriages and giddy love seemed like a dream he shouldn't have.

When he opened the email and read the first line, he sat back in his chair and shook his head.

Greetings from Palm Beach! I just got married!

Suddenly his stomach churned and his palms were damp. Marriage. Something he was taking seriously, but his mother, and father, didn't understand the concept of. It made him sick. He didn't even know she was seeing anyone, or that she'd left the state.

Again, he sat alone in his office and envied the life his cousins had had with their parents. Parents who knew what love was and how to handle a marriage. Why couldn't he get over this? Why did it bother him so much? Lydia was right. He needed counseling to get over his daddy issues—and his mommy issues.

Toward the end of the day, he pulled four beers from the cooler behind the bar and tucked them into his gym bag. He passed by each store front and waved at his sisters and cousins before pushing open the door to Jessie's store.

Inside she sat with a man and a woman, who held hands on

the white wicker couch. Jessie sat across from them, an album between them.

"Sorry to interrupt," he said as Jessie looked up at him.

She turned her attention back to the couple. "Why don't you look at these and I'll be just a moment." She stood and walked toward him, meeting him with a kiss to the cheek. "Are you headed to the gym?" she asked noting the bag.

"I'm going to stop by Jake's for a minute."

"Awesome, will you give something to Missy for me?" She turned around and picked up a small album from the table behind her. "She wanted to see a maternity session. She can bring this back to me anytime." She handed him the album.

"I will. I won't be too late."

"Take your time. I'm stopping by my parents' house after I'm done. My sister wants me to look at shoes." She winced, and he found humor in it. "I'll meet you at home. I love you."

And that was all he needed to hear. "I love you too."

CHAPTER 24

The drive out to Jake's garage had already calmed Todd's nerves. This was familiar to him, he thought. How many nights had he driven out there and sat with his brother while he fixed up his car for a race? There were a lot of fond memories in that garage.

Missy had seen him first and walked toward him, a wrench in her hand and a greasy smudge on her cheek.

"Where's your lady? I thought your days of coming out here solo were over," she teased as he pulled his bag from the passenger seat and shut the door.

"She's working. Just needed a few minutes and a few beers with my brother," Todd said as he kissed Missy on her clean cheek. "Here, Jessie wanted me to show you this."

He handed her the small album.

"Pearl wants me to do this," she said looking at the photos of pregnant women embracing their stomachs. "I don't know if this is me."

"So do it with your twist. Wear your racing suit and pose next to your car."

Her eyes lit up with that suggestion. "You're good at this too."

"No, Jessie has the eye. I just know you."

She smiled widely at him. "He's in with his car in the back. He's had a hard day. I think he'll be glad to see you."

Missy headed toward the office and Todd walked to the back garage where he heard his brother cussing at the engine he was working on.

"You must have gotten the same email I got this morning. Your mood sucks too," Todd called and Jake lifted his head to watch him walk closer. "I brought beer."

"Thank God." Jake tossed the wrench on the bench behind him and pulled over a turned over bucket and a stool for them to sit on as Todd pulled a beer for each of them from his bag. "She freaking ran away and got married? Again?"

"Yep, you got the same email."

Jake twisted off the top to the beer and drank down half of it before taking a breath. "She gives the sanctity of marriage a bad name. I've lost count. How many is this?"

"I don't know. One of them only lasted a month."

"That was number three," Jake confirmed.

"Right. Did you hear from Dad?"

Jake let out a grunt. "I try to avoid that with all my might. Anyone who bets on their kid to lose, doesn't deserve my time."

Todd wondered if they could get a discount if they went to counseling together for their combined daddy issues.

He twisted off the cap to his beer and took a long sip. "I suppose he'll call wanting to know all the details, or worse yet, he'll run off and get married just to one-up her."

Jake shook his head. "Except he'll steal the money from someone, make it seem as if it's owed to him, and then call again when he divorces whoever he conned into marrying him."

Todd thought he should laugh at his brother's assessment of the situation, but unfortunately he knew he was probably spot on.

In silence they finished their beers and Todd opened them each a second one.

"I'm moving in with Jessie," Todd announced his plans and watched as his brother smiled behind his beer.

"Sucker."

"Can't help it. I think she's the one."

"Missy told me that the day she met her."

"No kidding?"

Jake shook his head. "She doesn't get all girly on me often, but when she'd met Jessie, she came home all giddy, talking about you and your new woman."

"I don't think when she met Jessie we were an item yet."

"Oh, she just knew."

Hearing that made him want to run home to Jessie and plan a long future with her. And then he thought about his reason for sitting in his brother's garage drinking beer. There was a lot at stake when he thought about getting married. Sure, his brother was making it work, but maybe that was a fluke. They just didn't come from good stock, and that worried him.

Then he thought about Jessie's family. Her parents were happily married, and they'd gone through tremendous loss and still stayed together. Todd's parents hadn't been together since he was a child, they still couldn't have a civil conversation, and they hadn't been through anything like Jessie's parents.

He watched his brother take another drink of his beer and he wondered if Jake pondered these kinds of things when he'd fallen in love with Missy. Her family was equally unstable as theirs had been, and again, they were making it work.

"How do you guys make it work? The marriage thing?" he asked, and Jake lifted his head.

"She makes good coffee."

Todd laughed. "I mean it. Her family is messed up. Our family is messed up. How do either of you know what a solid marriage is supposed to be like?"

Jake narrowed his eyes on Todd. "Look at our aunt and uncle. Look at our grandparents. Sure, we come from the crazy side of the family, but we don't have to buy into it. I think if you love someone, you make it work."

And that was simple enough advice that Todd absolutely believed his brother. So their parents didn't believe in marriage. Hell, their mother didn't even care enough to have introduced her sons to the man she ran off and married. But that didn't have to reflect on him and Jessie.

He loved her, and in his mind, he was sure he was headed toward asking her to marry him.

But they'd agreed. They'd move in together first and then they could talk marriage, and he'd be ready.

Todd sat with his brother just a little longer and when he left, he thought maybe he'd call his mother and congratulate her on her marriage. He was sure that it would be over by the time they met her husband, but he could be the bigger person.

CHAPTER 25

Small heels. No heels. Chunky heels. Sandals.

They filled the table with different styles of shoes, and Jessie didn't like any of them. She still didn't want to be in the wedding party. Perhaps she just needed to be upfront about it. It really was her choice, wasn't it? She could provide her sister so much more support behind the camera.

"You'd prefer a flat, wouldn't you?" Carlie asked as she picked up one shoe.

"I look like a monster in heels."

Their mother flicked a hand in the air. "You never look like a monster. You're just tall."

"Too tall. Flats are the way to go for me."

Carlie nodded and gathered the three styles that were flat. "I suppose as long as the style matched, the heel wouldn't matter so much. Right?"

It was now or never, Jessie decided. "Listen, can we discuss this? I mean really discuss this?"

Carlie lifted her eyes to her sister. "That's what we're doing. We're discussing it."

"No, I mean me in your wedding. I know I'm your sister. And

I would be honored to be the witness that signs your marriage license, but I'm not comfortable being in the wedding. I would like to be your photographer. I would like to be the person who captures all the moments you will remember forever. I know you better than anyone in the world. I know how to translate what I know onto canvas. You wouldn't be sorry. I promise."

She could see the moisture filling her sister's eyes and it broke her heart.

Their mother took a breath. "Now, Jessica..."

Carlie held up a hand to stop their mother. Her lip quivered, and that broke Jessie's heart. "I never imagined you not in my wedding."

"I get that, but..."

"I know. I know. And you're right." She smiled though the tears began to stream down her cheeks. "I've never known anyone as talented as you, and you would capture the spirit of my wedding perfectly."

"I promise, you'd love them."

Carlie nodded. "I know I would. And if I force you to be in my wedding, you'll be miserable, and I'll have to hire a photographer I don't trust like I trust you." She wiped at her cheeks. "Okay, if that's what you really want."

"It is."

"Then you have to promise me you'll find someone to help you. I want you to capture the ceremony and all the special moments, but I want someone there to make sure you're captured in the pictures too. I'm not going to have a beautiful wedding album and not have my sister in there at all. You're still part of this wedding. You're still my most favorite human. I want you to be part of it all, even if you're not standing at the altar with me."

Now Jessie wiped away tears that had formed and escaped down her cheeks. "I'll find someone."

"Good." Carlie sucked in a breath and picked up one of the flats. "Now, do you like this one?"

Jessie exchanged looks with their mother before focusing back on Carlie. "Didn't we just settle this?"

"Yes. You're not going to walk down the aisle at my wedding or stand next to me. You're still my maid-of-honor and you're still going to be dressed. The last wedding I went to the photographers wore leggings and T-shirts. That is not going to happen here."

"I'll dress professionally. I would never—"

"Right. You'll be in your maid-of-honor dress, these flats," she said as she held up the shoe, "and in charge of capturing the moments I'll cherish forever."

Their mother covered her mouth with her fingers to hide the smile that had surfaced, and Jessie shook her head.

"Yes. Those flats would be best for me."

"Perfect."

When Carlie had said her goodbyes and their mother had walked her out the door, Jessie sat alone with their father at the kitchen table. He nursed a cup of tea and Jessie finished a glass of wine.

"I can't believe you were able to talk her into letting you out of the wedding," he said.

"Oh, I'm not out. I just don't have to stand up at the wedding. I'm still wearing that silly dress, and flats so I don't tower over everyone, so I don't know that I won this."

"Sure you did. You get to take the pictures, and that's what you wanted to do."

He was right. She'd have to consider it a win.

Her mother walked back into the kitchen, picked up her nearly full glass of wine, and joined them at the table.

"I think we're almost set. Pearl Walker has been so helpful in keeping your sister calm. She's like a bride whisperer."

"She's confident that they'll be married forever," Jessie said as she lifted her glass to sip.

"How does she know that?"

"Pearl. Her skill is knowing how long a marriage will last by how the bride treats those around her and the dress she picks. I can see how she's honed her skills. She sends me nearly all the couples that go through her store. I'm busy all the time with engagement photos and newborn sessions, from past customers of Pearl's that she keeps in touch with. But there are a few engagement sessions that I do where I'm thinking the couple doesn't even know each other."

Her mother laughed and sipped her wine. "What about you and Todd? Things are good with you?"

Jessie took in a deep breath and shifted a glance from her mother to her father, and then down to her wine. "Todd and I have decided to move in together. We're going to get our own place when my lease is up, and he's going to lease his place for the extra income."

Both of her parents lifted their drinks to their lips, sipped, and set their drinks down without saying a word.

So Jessie continued. "I love him. And he loves me. That much we know. We just feel like this is the next step, and who knows, maybe next year we'll plan another wedding. One I don't get to photograph."

Her mother reached her hand across the table and covered Jessie's. "We like him. And we know he's good to you. We assumed this was coming."

Then why were they making it so awkward, she wondered.

Her father leaned his elbows on the table and gave her a thoughtful look.

"Have you considered taking the money we offered you for your business?"

Jessie chuckled. "I don't need it. Because of the women I work around, I'm fully booked. Things are good. I've even been able to buy a few new props and a new lens."

"Then we'd like you to take the money and put it toward a home. It'll be a significant down payment, and if you and Todd are serious about where your relationship is going, then you can buy a good home to start a family in."

The tears threatened again, and Jessie didn't know what more to say, so she stood, walked around the table, and put an arm around each of her parents, pulling them in for a hug.

"I appreciate that. I love you."

CHAPTER 26

Jessie pulled into the driveway just as Todd pulled up on the street and parked his truck. He stepped out and walked toward her while she gathered her things.

"What timing, huh?" she asked, slinging her bag over her shoulder, grabbed the two grocery bags from the back seat, and closed the door to her car with her hip.

"Fate?"

"Could be."

Todd walked to her and leaned in to kiss her gently on the lips.

"How is your brother?"

"Fine. Your sister and parents?"

"Fine as well. Let's go inside and make some dinner. I'm starving. Then you can fill me in on your visit and I can fill you in on mine."

He nodded, but she wasn't sure he was too eager to share.

Todd took the grocery bags she carried and followed her through the front door and back to the kitchen where he set the groceries on the counter.

"Did your sister decided on shoes?" he asked as he pulled the items from the bag.

"Graciously enough, she's allowing me a pair of flats so I don't tower over all the guests," she said with a laugh. "But I won't be in the wedding itself."

A line formed between his brows. "What does that mean? You're not in the wedding anymore?"

"I asked her to let me be the photographer. It would mean more to me than to be up at the altar with her, just standing there. I'm better at capturing her moment. She finally agreed. I will still be her maid-of-honor, but I get to be the photographer."

Todd moved to her, wrapping his arm around her waist. "And that's what you want?"

"It's what I want."

"Then it sounds like everything worked out for you."

She shrugged. "I still have to wear that fancy dress and those flat shoes."

"And you'll be the most beautiful woman at the wedding. But don't tell your sister I said that."

"I wouldn't dream of it," she promised, leaning in to kiss him softly. "And what about you? How is Jake?"

Todd turned from her, pulling a chair from the table and sitting. "Our mother got married," he said, raking his fingers through his hair. "She sent us both an email. Short and sweet, just telling us she'd gotten married in Palm Beach."

Jessie pulled out the chair next to him and sat down, facing him. "She's happy, right?"

He shrugged. "No idea. I didn't even know she'd left town. Nor did I know she'd been seeing anyone."

"So you don't know the man?"

"Nope. She didn't even include his name in her email."

Jessie reached for his hand and held it in hers. "I'm sorry."

"For what? Because my mother doesn't consider her family when she makes decisions? She's never has."

"You're upset?"

Todd stood and paced. "I am. But I'm not. I mean why do I care? If she wants to get married and divorced again, that's not my problem, right? Of course, when my father hears about this, then he'll probably marry the next woman he sleeps with too."

"Todd," she said his name in warning.

"This is how my family works. Marriage doesn't mean a damn thing."

Now Jessie stood to meet him eye-to-eye. "That's how your parents work. Your family is bigger than your parents."

"Yes, but this is how I was brought up. You love for a moment and then you just give the hell up."

"Is that how you work?"

"I don't know. I've never been in a long relationship that looked like it might lead to marriage."

"Well, what about this one?" She motioned her hand between them. "We're moving in together. That's the first step toward marriage, right? Isn't that what we agreed?"

"Maybe it's a dumb idea. I mean, now you see how things work."

"No, I see how things work for your parents. That doesn't mean that's how things will work between us."

"But I don't know that."

"Really?" She threw up her hands. "You don't know that? You just assume that because your parents are messed up, then you are too? I'm glad you're letting me know. What a waste of time for me to move in with you only for you to get scared and run off."

She turned, finished with the conversation they were having, walked to the bedroom and slammed the door.

· · ·

TODD DROPPED into the chair he'd occupied earlier, resting his head in his hands. This was exactly what he was afraid of. His parents' messed up ideals would lose him his own happiness.

Pressing his fingers to his eyes, he thought of Jessie's parents and what they must have gone through when they lost their son. Hadn't she said her father turned to drinking and her mother turned to prayer? Yet, somehow they met in a common place and continued on.

She was right. This had nothing to do with him. He didn't decide for his parents. His brother was making his marriage work, and Todd was throwing away a good thing.

No, he was having a setback. He wouldn't let Jessie out of his life, and he wasn't done fighting for her.

He stood and made his way down the hallway to the bedroom.

With his hand on the knob, he realized the door was locked, and how could he blame her? But he wasn't finished, so he wasn't walking away.

"Jessie, open the door. I want to talk."

"The reason I locked the door is that I don't want to talk." Her words were muffled.

"I'm not leaving. I'm stupid to think I'm anything like my parents. I let that take hold of me too often. C'mon, open the door."

There was silence for a moment, but then the lock clicked and Jessie pulled open the door, slightly, still standing with her hand on the knob.

"The door is open. Now what?"

"Jessie, I'm sorry. I didn't mean—"

"If you're sorry then you'll take tonight to think about what you said to me. If your parents, and their marriage habits consume you, then take some time to consider moving in with me. I'm not here for a short run. I'm here for the long haul, but not if you're just going to give it up in a moment of confusion."

She didn't move from the doorway, and he wondered if she would step back and let him in. Her eyes focused on him, and he could only stand there.

"So why don't you go home. Let's not be together tonight. When you know how you want to proceed, then come find me, but not tonight."

And with that, she closed and locked the door again.

CHAPTER 27

$\mathcal{S}$leep hadn't come to Todd, so he'd brewed a pot of coffee at five in the morning and headed into work. It wasn't like he didn't have plenty to keep his mind occupied. Spring was upon them and that meant every Saturday through July was booked with a wedding, including Jessie's sister's.

Todd inventoried the bar, made a linen order and updated the wine order. He emailed Susan a change in a menu that had come through, and shot another email to Pearl with a question from a potential bride.

Looking at his watch, he'd noted that he'd been working for nearly three hours already. Without windows in his office, there was no sign of sunlight, so he brought up the cameras that surrounded the *Bridal Mecca* and took an inventory there.

Nichole had opened the salon that morning. Audrey would arrive around ten. Gia's store was still dark. She, too, wouldn't open until ten. His sister Pearl's car was in her designated space. She wouldn't see her first bride until ten, but assuredly she'd been in her office since eight. That was her schedule and how she worked every day.

As he watched the cameras, he saw Jessie's car pull up in the lot. He zoomed in.

She stepped out of her car, pulling out the bags she carried to and from her studio to home and back. He knew there were snacks, magazines she used for inspiration, a bottle of water, and a change of clothes buried inside. More than once she'd had a kid get something on her during a photo shoot, but he didn't want to know what.

He watched as she reached back inside and pulled out a tray with two coffees on it. Wasn't it funny that suddenly he wanted another cup of coffee?

With her hip, Jessie shut the door and then stood there for another moment. She looked up at the camera that was perched atop the roof, lifted the tray, and then walked to her studio.

The tension that had knotted up in Todd's shoulders released. Another trait he'd inherited from his parents was holding on to a grudge—and that was obvious by his sleeping alone last night. Jessie, on the other hand, believed in sleeping off the mad and starting over—also obvious by the coffee gesture.

Todd tidied up his desk, turned off his computer screen, and took the outside loop around the building, which would take two minutes longer, to get to her studio.

By the time he approached her door, she'd set down her bags, turned on the lights, and stood there with a cup of coffee in each hand.

"Just the way you like it. A little cream, a little sugar, a little flavor," she said as he walked through the door.

He hesitated for a moment. "We're okay?"

Jessie narrowed her eyes on him. "This is hot. Can you take it?"

He hurried inside and took the paper cup from her hand, then turned to kiss her gently, which she accepted.

Jessie sipped from her cup. "You're not used to just letting things play out, are you?"

"No. Is that how this works?"

She sipped again. "We will talk about it. I'm not marrying a man who freaks out every time his parents do something that ultimately doesn't affect him."

And that's what had happened. His mother ran off and got married and he'd taken it as a personal slap. In fact, the only time it would matter would be when she divorced the man and needed to complain about it. He knew there was a process.

"You're right to say that. I didn't handle myself very well yesterday."

"And that's understandable. But you're not your mother and you're not your father. You're very careful to refrain from taking on their ways. I've seen it in you. I've heard that from you. I've talked to your sisters. And I know how you really are around your family—the other side of the family. I'm willing to give you time to mourn what your mother did, but I'm not willing to watch you crumble under it."

Her words were firm and thought out. She'd either believed this the entire time, or she'd rehearsed. Either way, she was right.

Todd set his coffee on the table behind Jessie, then took her cup and did the same.

Lifting his hands to her face, he gazed into her eyes. There were signs of sleeplessness and tears there.

"I'm truly sorry for my attitude yesterday. It does not reflect on how I feel moving forward. I still want to live with you, and when we know that's perfect, then I want to talk about marrying you."

"It will never be perfect, and you can't expect that."

"I don't. But I know that it's what I want and I'll work to make it as perfect as possible. I love you, and I never want to lose you over my fears of being like my parents. I look at Jake and Missy, who started out as enemies, and now have this wonderful life, and I think I deserve that. And I know they work at it. Her family is equally as messed up as mine. I should be far ahead, because your family understands the bonds of marriage and the true meaning of family. What I need to remember is that by creating a family with you, then I have them as family, too."

Her eyes welled with tears. "Yeah. Remember that. You get them and they really like you."

He lowered his hands to pull her into him and hold her tight. "And I really like them"

Her breath was warm against his neck and her tears wet against his cheek. As she stepped back, he lifted his hand to brush away the tears that lingered.

"Thank you for the coffee—just the way I like it," he breathed.

"You're welcome. Now, get out of here. I have a consultation in twenty minutes. I have to fix my makeup and set up."

Todd pressed a gentle kiss to her lips. "Time for lunch?"

"I have a cake smash at eleven, before the baby's nap I'm told. So I'll just eat what I brought. Then I have another consultation at three."

"Dinner at home then?"

"Sounds good."

"I'll cook and will wait for you. Are you going to the gym after work?"

Her lips turned up in a smile. "I'd planned to."

"That gives me more time." He kissed her again. "I love you."

"I love you, too. Now go."

Todd picked up his coffee, gave her a wink, and went back to work feeling like a brand-new man.

CHAPTER 28

The rest of their week was normal, and for that Todd was grateful. He flung his gym bag over his shoulder and headed into the YMCA where he would work out, shower, watch Jessie play basketball, and then join her and the rest of the players for a beer.

It had become as much part of his routine as living with her and sharing morning coffee.

Finn waved at him as Todd emerged from the locker room and headed for the elliptical to warm up. Finn would often warm up before a game with some weights, or some social time as Todd had noted was the case.

Jessie had opted for a swim to warm up, and he'd caught sight of her as she emerged from the pool. Her long legs toned, her arms sculpted, and her hair longer than when they'd met. He knew that she couldn't see into the gym, but he could see her, so he enjoyed the view.

Todd moved on to the free weights, then did some leg presses. By the time it fatigued him, he realized it was nearly time for them to play. He headed for the showers, emerging as they tipped the ball in Big Finn's direction.

Todd set his bag in the corner and noticed that Jessie's parents were seated in the small section of bleachers. He waved as her mother looked in his direction and then he walked over to sit with them.

"It's nice to see you, Todd," her mother smiled up at him and her father extended his hand and Todd shook it.

"Can't miss Sunday night basketball," he said as he watched Jessie take the ball down the court and shoot a three-pointer.

She looked up at him and he winked as her father clapped and cheered her on.

"Have you two found a house yet?" Carol Hanson asked.

"Not yet. We've been busy. We will carve out some time next week to look."

"I hope you find a nice one. A good starter. I know that what we gave her should be a good down payment."

Todd knew his expression didn't match the words that came in response. "I think so. And thank you."

"Oh, our pleasure. She wouldn't let us give it to her for her business, so we thought this would be the next best thing."

Todd nodded and turned his attention back to the game. It seemed as if in their squabble the other day, Jessie had forgotten to mention that her parents were footing the down payment on their house. Were they going to buy a house to live in? He'd thought they would lease.

Suddenly the air in the gym grew even more stagnant, and he'd like to have left and gotten some fresh air into his lungs, but he wouldn't do that. No, his days of running out when he didn't understand a situation, or didn't like it, were over. They'd have this conversation after the game, beers, and dinner. And it would be a conversation, not some crazy argument that had them sleeping in different locations.

Jessie shot another three-pointer, and her father rose to his feet and cheered. She blew him a kiss and Todd pushed back any pang of jealousy. His father would have bet against him in a game, had he bothered to show up, but not hers. And that was okay, because Todd knew if he were out there playing with them, her father would cheer for him, too.

And just like that, it hit him. They'd talked about it, and now he knew it. The people sitting next to him would be his family if he married Jessie. They would love him and coddle him too. Hell, all he was doing was moving in with her and they were putting the down payment on the house.

He was one of them, and he hadn't taken the time to accept that and appreciate that.

Warmth spread through his chest, and he wanted to grab the couple next to him and hug them tightly. Instead, he rose to his feet and cheered too.

Jessie laughed and brushed them off with a flick of her hand.

As they threw the ball in from the sidelines, Todd and her father sat back down and watched as Jessie stood in front of Finn, who towered over her, his face dripping with sweat.

He could hear her toying with the man as she caught the ball and slipped under his arm and around him.

Finn's balance was compromised, and Todd saw the large man begin to fall toward Jessie. She must have seen it too because she moved, right before he would have taken her down with him.

Jessie threw the ball to her teammate, who took it down the court and through the hoop, but her attention was still on Big Finn, who lay on the court, face down.

"Finn!" Jessie yelled as she fell to her knees beside him.

Within seconds, the players on the court were surrounding him, rolling him to his back.

Todd heard her voice again, "Finn!"

More words were shouted.

"He's not breathing."

"Heart attack."

"CPR."

Carol grabbed his arm. "What's happening?"

"I think he had a heart attack," Todd said as he pulled his phone from his pocket and called 9-1-1, just as he noticed Jessie's father doing too.

Jessie had her hands planted on Finn's chest, and another woman was poised right above him. As Jessie pressed down on his chest, the other woman would breathe into his mouth when Jessie would stop. They continued this process until one of the Y employees came in with the machine off the wall.

Todd was paralyzed. Carol's grip on his arm grew tighter. The chaos only ensued as the paramedics arrived and took over. The players on the court backed away, but Jessie knelt next to him, her hand in his.

"C'mon, Finn. You owe me a beer," she said, and Todd could see the tears falling.

The paramedics lifted him onto the stretcher and hurried him out to the waiting ambulance.

Todd hurried to Jessie, standing on the court now, watching them push Finn through the door.

"He's going to be okay. You all got to him fast enough," he said hoping he was speaking the truth.

"I have to go. I have to be there."

"Okay. We'll go," he agreed.

"He was there for my brother. I have to be there for him. I have to be there for Finn."

Todd wrapped his arm around her waist and helped her to the bleachers to sit while he gathered her things. Her mother was clinging to her now, and her father enveloped them both in his arms.

Family, he reminded himself. This was how family acted. He was part of this family now.

Todd gathered her bag, pulling her sweatshirt out so he could drape it over her shoulders.

As a family, they headed to Todd's truck and all of them went to the hospital to hold vigil for Big Finn—another honorary member of the Hanson family.

CHAPTER 29

*L*uckily the hospital wasn't far and Todd pulled up just after the ambulance.

Before he even had the truck in park, Jessie opened the door and ran for the entrance to the emergency room. She wanted to be with him. At least she could start giving his information to the doctors.

Carl, who had been on the court with them, had called Finn's son and ex-wife. But aside from them, his friends were his only family.

"They're working on him. Can I get you anything?" The lady at the desk asked as she handed Jessie a clipboard with paperwork to fill out.

"I'd like to see him."

"They're getting his situation under control. I will let them know you're here."

That wasn't what Jessie wanted at all. She wanted to be holding the big oaf's hand. She wanted to tell him that she couldn't do it without him. She needed him to know that she was sorry for all the times they'd collided, or bumped, or tripped over each other.

The tears had begun to well in her eyes enough she couldn't read the forms.

A hand came to her shoulder, and she turned to see a fuzzy image of Todd standing over her.

"Hey, sweetheart." He sat down next to her. "What do we have here?" He took the board from her.

"His papers," she began to sob. "I can at least help fill out his papers."

Todd pressed a kiss to her cheek. "Do you know all of this stuff?"

She nodded and handed him her phone. It was open to an email Finn had once sent her after an emergency visit for a twisted ankle. "He thought maybe, since I was always with him when he fell down, I should know everything." She looked up at Todd. "God, do you think he knew something like this was going to happen?"

Todd lifted a hand to her wet cheek and held it there for a moment. "He seems like the kind of guy who wants to cover all his bases." Todd took the phone and held it next to the clipboard. "Would you like me to help you with this?"

What she wanted was to be with Finn. Instead, she nodded, grateful for Todd's help.

They filled out the paperwork, the best they could, and when Todd walked back to the desk to return it, a nurse came from the back and moved directly to Jessie.

"Are you the one who came in with Finnegan McBride?"

It took her a moment to connect his full name, but Jessie nodded. "Yes. Is he okay? I want to see him."

The nurse smiled. "He's stable. Are you family?"

Jessie shook her head. "No. Dear friends. His family isn't here yet."

"I'll take you back. But when his family arrives—"

"I get it," she said following the nurse back through the forbidden doors.

It took everything she had inside of her not to crack again the moment she saw him. The larger-than-life man looked tiny in the bed, covered in wires and blankets. A monitor beeped to the side of him, and his eyes were closed.

"He'll be in and out, but we're keeping him calm. They're going to admit him and, keep him for observation, and run some tests."

"It was a heart attack, right?"

"Yes."

Jessie kept her purse hugged to her front, as if it were a comforting blanket from childhood. Her eyes were fixed on Finn, and she wondered how much pain could fill one's chest before it was critical, because hers ached horribly.

There was comfort in hearing the constant beep next to her. He'd survived.

"Hey," his raspy voice broke the otherwise silent air in the room.

"Hey, big guy. Jesus, you've given me a scare."

A small smile pushed up one corner of his mouth. "Were you the one kissing me, or beating me?"

Jessie wiped away the tears that stained her cheeks and let out a small laugh. "Beating you."

He nodded slightly and let his eyes close again.

At least his humor was still intact, she thought as he drifted to sleep, the rhythm of his heart keeping her company.

Thirty minutes after she'd been escorted back to him, the curtain pushed to the side and his ex-wife and son walked through.

His ex-wife gasped when she saw him, and that seemed to wake him enough to look up at her.

"Hey, lover," he said to her, and she shook her head. "Wanna dance?"

That caused the woman to laugh, covering her mouth as she

did so while tears streamed down her cheeks. "Seriously? You're joking?"

Finn managed a shrug before he looked up at his son. "Junior, you're looking mighty big."

The boy, now thirteen, if Jessie remembered correctly, stared at his father with wide eyes.

"Jessie, remember Junior?" he asked.

Jessie nodded. "You're taller than I remember."

The boy looked at her and nodded, but otherwise was silent, still in shock from seeing his father laying there.

"Roster him for my next game," Big Finn joked weakly.

"Will do," she promised as she stood. "It looks like you're in good hands now, Finn. I'll see you when they've sprung you. Maybe you could be a quiet spectator for a bit."

He had enough energy to roll his eyes at her. "I owe you a beer."

Jessie chuckled as she leaned in and kissed his cheek. "Damn straight you do. Take care of you," she said softly in his ear.

"I'm in good hands. She'll dote on me," he said looking up at his ex-wife who clearly still loved the oaf.

Todd paced the waiting area while Jessie's parents worked on a crossword puzzle from a three-year-old magazine.

A few others had come after the game to check up on Finn, and they waited, scattered around the room.

When Jessie emerged, Todd went to her, enveloping her in his arms.

"Well? How is he?"

She laid her hand gently on his chest. "Ornery," she joked. "I think he's going to be fine. His ex-wife and son are back there now."

"You talked to him?"

Jessie nodded. "He owes me a beer."

Todd pulled her to him and held tightly as she let the rest of her tears fall. As she sobbed, he breathed her in. God, he loved this woman who could be tough enough to sport a black eye with humor, and soft enough to crumble when her heart ached.

CHAPTER 30

$\mathcal{E}$very morning after they released Finn from the hospital, Jessie would stop by his house just to make sure he was doing okay.

His ex-wife had stayed with him for the first week, but as Finn admitted, she'd quickly remembered why they'd divorced.

"God, I still love her, and she loves me. Isn't it interesting that two people can be as addicted to one another as we are, but can't make a marriage work?" he asked as he turned down the volume on his TV so that the voice of the woman on the news had disappeared. "At least we get along when Finn Junior is around. We might not live together, but at least he knows he's loved by both of us."

The very thought of that made Jessie sad for Todd. Obviously, his parents had been so selfish, he didn't feel that love on either side.

"Do you have to work at that?" Jessie asked, taking a bite of the piece of toast Finn had offered her when she'd arrived.

"What, at making him feel loved? No. He is loved."

"I mean working together. How do you do that?"

He lifted his brows in thought. "It's just the right thing to do," he said matter-of-factly. "I suppose we work on it in our own way. We never fought in front of him. Our fights were ours, not his. I don't say anything bad about her in front of him, and vice-versa. Those things are between her and me, not him."

There was a lightness in her chest when he spoke about a woman he loved and couldn't live with.

"You're an amazing man," she said as she stood and kissed him on the cheek.

"Not amazing enough. I can't keep a wife."

"That's not what classifies you as a good man. I have to get to work now."

She pulled her purse up over her shoulder.

"How's your little business going?" he asked.

"Wonderful. I fell into the right place. Those women I work around feed each other business and lift one another up like nothing I've ever seen. And I've been around a lot of supportive people in my life."

Finn smiled. "I'm proud of you."

"Thanks."

"I mean it. You've always been a go-getter, and this is no different. And that guy?"

Now Jessie smiled and she could feel it light through her. "I love him. I think I want to marry him."

"And that's in the plans?"

She shrugged. "We're getting a place together, and then we'll go from there."

"Smart girl. I suppose had my wife and I lived together first, we would have realized that we can't live with each other. Of course, we probably wouldn't have our son, and that would be a shame. No matter how it happens, you make it work."

"Don't forget you owe me a beer," she reminded him as she walked to the door.

"For the rest of my life—which I still have thanks to you."

Jessie blew him a kiss and let herself out.

~*~

MARCH GAVE INTO APRIL, and the entire *Bridal Mecca* geared up for spring and the upcoming busy season.

May and June meant weddings—four or five a week in the reception hall, and more when it came to dresses, bouquets, hairstyles, and photo sessions.

Jessie worked with her mother, and her sister's best friend, to plan a bridal shower and bachelorette party. She'd taken in all the knowledge she could possibly collect from the women she worked around, and she thought she had a good grasp on the best venue, party favors, gifts, and decorations out there. With her sister's wedding in June, they planned to hold the shower in early May on the back patio of her parents' home.

After all the stores had closed on a rainy April afternoon, Jessie sat in Pearl's store with the women of the *Bridal Mecca*, and they enjoyed a new bottle of Italian wine Gia had brought in and a delightful meat and cheese tray which looked like Susan had slaved over.

It had become a custom to gather at least once a month, if not more, to discuss business and family—and Jessie was part of both.

Audrey was the last to arrive, and she locked the door behind her as she entered the bridal store. "Phillip just called me. Those guys who were breaking into businesses broke into Juanita's Beauty Shop a few miles away. She's on vacation, so the store is closed. No one knew anything happened until a fire broke out."

Gia choked on her sip of wine. "Fire?"

Audrey perched herself on the arm of the sofa and nodded as she picked up a cracker and a piece of cheese. "I guess this time they went in, couldn't find any money, so they dumped out all of her chemicals and left a curling iron in the middle of it all. I guess it finally either shorted out and sparked, or the chemicals got hot enough to combust. I don't know, but it's a total loss."

Pearl crossed a leg over the other and rested her wrists on her knee. "How do they know it's the same guys?"

"Liquor store next door has footage. They got some smoke and water damage too."

Pearl shook her head. "I guess we need to keep vigilant. We're wired. Todd has turned over every piece of surveillance he's had on them. All of our stores are wired into that system. We make a pact here and now. No one works alone or leaves alone."

The group of women all agreed.

Pearl looked toward Jessie. "You come and go with Todd. If he doesn't have anything going on, he can sit while you work. And if he gives you any lip on that, I'll handle it."

Jessie chuckled. "I'm sure he wouldn't fuss over that at all. He's rather protective of all of us."

Pearl lifted her head toward Audrey. "Did Phillip say they had any leads yet? I mean we've seen the guys come and go, but no specific car or motive has been found, right?"

Audrey shrugged, lifting another cracker to her mouth. "They'd had no incidents for about a month, and then this. He says they don't know who is doing it. They're in and out before anyone knows. There are no clear shots of their faces."

Gia pressed a hand to her chest. "I am not comforted by this."

Pearl lifted a manicured finger. "And that's why we stay vigilant and work as a team. We're fierce women who stand for one another. That could be something a bad guy doesn't like. We've been there, some of us," she said as she looked around the room. "We're all still here. No one takes one of our businesses or one of us for granted."

She put that perfectly manicured hand in the center of their circle, and each woman put their hand on top.

Sisterhood at its finest, Jessie thought as she put in her hand and Audrey put hers on top of it.

CHAPTER 31

*A*fter three more break-ins and no suspects apprehended, the women of the *Bridal Mecca* were on full alert. The vandals had hit the coffee shop, the barber shop—again, and this time Ella, of all people, had a broken window.

Each morning, after Todd had done a full walk through of Jessie's studio, checked all the doors to the businesses in the building, and took a physical inventory of the reception hall, he opened the recorded images from that night's camera footage. If there was any foot traffic whatsoever, he'd send it to Phillip.

Phillip had decided that the person causing all the damage was just out to damage things. The items they took were small, and it was infrequent. They'd set fire to a bush outside the ice cream store, but a bar patron had seen that, and extinguished it.

The Walker family had fielded its share of crazy people. Todd's sister and cousin had been attacked by a mentally unstable police officer in Phillip Smythe's office. His sister-in-law's own brother had attacked Jake. His cousin Russell had been run off the road, and the list went on and on. Should they assume they were being targeted? No. Out of all the businesses in town, their end of the main street had been the least messed with.

The fires were new though, and that had Todd working with the landscaper to make sure that the bushes around the building were well watered. The last thing they needed were any dry shrubs going up in flames.

Todd tended to his orders and when his Skype account rang on his computer, he opened it to see Lydia's smiling face.

"What a nice surprise!" he cheered, and she laughed.

"I Skype you every Wednesday."

"Eh, it still feels special. What's new, boss?"

Lydia held up an airline ticket and Todd's mouth went dry.

"No way," he drawled squinting his eyes on the screen. "You're coming home?"

"I'm scared to death," she admitted, and her voice shook.

"Why? Everyone here is dying to see you."

"I just want everything to be normal, you know. I want it to be like the day before all the shit hit the fan last year. I just want to walk into my office and have your sisters stop to say good morning and go on with their days."

"It's not going to happen."

"Yeah. I've been working through that. Don't tell anyone, okay? I want it to be a surprise."

Todd wrinkled up his nose and let out a huff. "Seriously? You want me to keep a secret?"

"I know you can do it."

"You're right. Damnit!"

She laughed. "I'm almost home."

"I can't wait."

Lydia's smile intensified. "Okay, fill me in. What's up today?"

Todd pulled out the legal pad he kept his notes on and read them off to Lydia as he did every week. He crossed off the things she approved, made notes on changes, and took more notes with her bright ideas.

· · ·

~*~

JESSIE SORTED through the mail as she stood at the counter in her kitchen. There was an envelope from the agency that managed the lease on her house.

Resting a hip against her counter, she opened it.

"What's that?" Todd asked, giving a nod to the yellow paper in her hand as he opened the refrigerator and pulled out the salad and dressing they'd prepared for dinner.

"The notice that my lease is coming due." She blew out a breath. "I don't know when we'll find time to look for a new place to live. I had no idea I would be as busy as I am. Do you know how many weddings are held in the spring?" she asked looking at the letter.

Todd looked up at her, his hands still full, and an eyebrow raised. "You saw my schedule for the next three months, right? I'm not home a Friday or Saturday night until July."

Jessie let out a laugh and tossed the letter on the counter. "Right. I guess we'd better decide how we'll handle all this."

Todd set the salad and dressing on the table and turned to her. "I hadn't given this much thought, but the night Finn had his heart attack, your parents said something to me I think we'd better discuss."

Her eyes went wide, and she pulled a chair from the kitchen table and sat down. "Damn, we sure haven't talked in a few weeks, have we?"

He laughed as he took a seat. "No. Your mom said they gave you money for a down payment?"

Tears began to well in her eyes. "I meant to talk to you about this. Please don't think I was hiding it from you."

"I don't think that. That night was unexpected for everyone." He took her hand in his, and lifted it to his lips, pressing a kiss to her fingers. "So, we're thinking of buying a house?"

"I don't know what we're thinking." She wiped at her eyes. "Buying a house is a big step. It's not a lease that will end."

"I'm not going anywhere, Jess. A mortgage isn't a life sentence."

"It's so final," she said and then look up into his eyes. "I don't mean that badly."

"Maybe we should rethink this. We've decided to move in together. We've thrown around the what comes after that idea." He ran his thumb over her knuckles. "You know, we've been living together, mostly, for the past three months. Minus that one night when I went back to Lydia's, I've been here."

She nodded slowly. "You have."

"Buying a house won't change what we've already been doing."

"Right."

Todd slid from the chair, and down to the floor on one knee, still holding Jessie's hand in his. Her breath caught as he smiled up at her.

"I want to live with you forever. In a house, in a car, on a boat," he laughed. "I don't care where it is. Home will be wherever you are. So Jessica Hanson, will you marry me?"

This was not what she'd expected. This wasn't in her plan, was it? Did she have a plan?

She stared at him, unable to talk.

They'd talked about this. They'd planned for this, even if they didn't say when.

She swallowed hard and Todd lifted his brows since she hadn't accepted or declined his offer.

He'd understand if she said no, because he'd know she had questions, or thoughts, or—damnit, she thought too much.

This man, who was so afraid of becoming his parents was on one knee asking her to live the rest of her life as his wife—a Walker. She was making him suffer, and she realized that when she saw the bead of sweat form in his hairline.

"Todd..."

He shook his head. "I'm sorry. I should have—"

"Yes. Yes. Yes, of course I'll marry you."

Her heart raced as he lifted his eyes to meet hers. He hesitated a moment before the smile returned to his lips. "You'll marry me?"

"I'll marry you."

"You want to marry me?"

"Oh, God!" She slid from her chair and met him kneeling on the floor. "You took me by surprise."

"That's kind of the point."

"I don't care where we live either. But I want to be your wife, your partner, your everything. I want to be Mrs. Todd Walker."

Just saying the name aloud made her giddy with anticipation and just a little dizzy. She closed her eyes to regain her composure.

When she opened them again, he was smiling widely.

"I love you."

"I love you, too, Todd. I really do. Oh, God. We're really going to do this? We're going to get married?"

Now he laughed, still holding her hand in his. "We're going to get married."

"I want simple."

"Anything you want."

"I don't want a big wedding party. I don't want lots of flowers or shoes that match dresses. I think your sister eloping was a great idea."

She wouldn't do it. It wouldn't be fair to her family to not be there, but knowing that Pearl, who made her living making sure everyone's special day was perfect, hadn't even wanted a fancy wedding—that made her even happier to be a Walker.

Todd looked down at her hand. "I'd thought I'd do this in a much grander moment and have a ring."

Jessie hadn't even noticed he didn't present her with a ring.

"I don't need one."

"Oh, yes you do," he shot back. "I'll let you pick it out though. Something tells me the one I'd buy you wouldn't be right."

"I'm not that difficult."

"Nope, you're not. But you deserve the right one." He shifted, so he was on both knees, and he pulled her to him. "So this is what the rest of them felt."

"Who?"

"My brother, sisters, cousins. This was when they knew that everything would be better—together."

"We're engaged."

"We are. The last of the Walkers is off the market."

She laughed again. "I don't want to eat dinner," she said lifting her fingers into his hair.

"No?"

"Let's go celebrate, alone, in the dark."

"I'm finding I'm not as hungry as I thought."

Todd stood. Offering his hand to Jessie, he helped her off the floor.

"You're the most beautiful fiancée any man has ever had."

"Fiancée," she said the word and then pressed her hand to her chest. "I like the sound of that."

"So do I."

CHAPTER 32

They'd left the house early enough to stop and have breakfast on the way to work, since they had never made it back to finishing their dinner.

When they reached the *Bridal Mecca* they parted with a kiss, and Todd left her at her studio and walked onward to his own office, but not without stopping by Pearl's store first.

He noticed her startle when he walked through the door. "I thought you all had a pact. No one alone in the building."

She shook her head at him. "I have eleven—eleven brides coming in today. Sunshine and I will be so busy we won't have time to pee."

The comment took him off guard and he laughed.

"Still. Until they catch those guys…"

"Who haven't broken into anything for a while."

"They took a break last time too."

"Todd, I can take care of myself. So if you don't mind. I have a million things I have to do before Sunshine gets here and we have wall-to-wall brides. God forbid we have any walk-ins."

He knew she didn't mean that. There was nothing his sister liked more than to be so busy her head spun.

"Fine, but I wanted to tell you something before I go. I did a little thing last night."

~*~

SELF-EMPLOYMENT DIDN'T COME with a nine-to-five schedule. Jessie understood that. But when she looked at her watch and it said five-fifteen, there was a moment where she always felt like giving herself a pat on the back because she'd successfully had another great day in business.

Todd would be another hour, which gave her time to edit the sessions she'd shot the day before. She promised herself to always be timely when handling a family's special moments, especially when the children were little. She'd known photographers that took so long processing the pictures that the kids didn't look the same when they got their photos back.

Jessie startled when she heard the chime over her door. Usually she would have locked the door and turned off the lights while she worked in the back of her studio.

"Jessie, are you back there?" Pearl's voice filled the small space.

A smile came to Jessie's lips. "Yes. I'll be right there." She let out a breath and let her heart rate settle.

She saved the screen she was working on and grinned down at her work. The photo of a sweet one-year-old in a bathtub with big pink, plastic bubbles melted her heart. Now that she and Todd had made their relationship permanent—in the most permanent of ways—she found that every picture she edited tugged at her heart a little more. It was silly. She'd been engaged for one day, and wedding details weren't on her mind, but babies were.

Jessie turned off her work light and walked out to the front of her studio only to instantly raise her hands to her face in sheer surprise at every Walker woman standing there.

Pearl held a cake, Glenda a tray of sandwiches, and Susan a bottle of champagne.

Audrey held a bouquet of balloons, and Bethany a bouquet. Gia, Missy, Ella, Nichole, and Chelsea had also walked in with their arms full of gifts and bags.

"What is all of this?" Jessie felt the tears spill from her eyes and down her cheeks.

"My brother told me some amazing news this morning, and as far as I'm concerned he did a horrible job proposing. So, we decided you needed more attention. This is your engagement party."

Jessie pressed her fingers to her trembling lips, and the tears poured again when the door opened and her mother and sister walked through it.

She moved to them as the Walker women assembled their party.

"You're here too," she gleefully whispered in their ears as she held them both close.

"Todd came over this morning and told us what he'd done. He'd wanted to apologize because he had wanted to ask for our blessing first. But he has it."

Jessie turned to her sister. "I didn't want to say anything until after you got married. I didn't want to steal your spotlight."

"You won't." Carlie gave Jessie's hand a squeeze. "We have different styles. But you win in the department of in-laws."

They all turned to look at the women who fussed over details and setting up the perfect, impromptu party.

Jessie's chest filled with love. This was her family now, and who would have imagined that when she escorted her sister to the bridal shop that morning in early February that this would be where she'd have landed herself—in love with a man whose family loved her too.

For the next three hours, the Walker women surrounded Jessie, her mother, and her sister celebrating what was to come. The engagement gifts were thoughtful and precious. How they could even have planned everything on such short notice was beyond her. Then again, she decided that they'd had many years to perfect such things. The Walker women worked as a team, and as a new member arrived, she was welcomed and given her tasks. The thought made her chuckle. What would be the next situation where the Walker women would assemble, and what would be her duty?

As she looked around the room at the proud women, she wondered if Todd would tell his mother of their engagement. A bit of sadness crept into her chest when she thought about it. But at that moment Glenda let out a laugh that caught her attention. No, she decided, Todd probably wouldn't tell his mother much about their relationship. But he would share everything with his aunt who doted on him like a loving mother should. She was the woman who had truly made Todd into the man he was, and Jessie knew that.

They told stories about Todd growing up, and Jessie found that he'd been a quiet child.

"He might have been quiet, but he was the troublemaker deep inside," Pearl said. "He could come up with all the good ideas. Of course, he wouldn't follow through with them and he'd be quietly in his room when the rest of us carried out his devilish plans."

Glenda roared with laughter again. "I don't think his butt ever saw the end of a paddle."

"No, by the time anyone would have gotten through us to him, their hands would have been tired anyway."

They all laughed and Jessie's mother gave her hand a squeeze.

This was what she'd always wanted and never knew it. She couldn't wait to be Mrs. Todd Walker.

CHAPTER 33

Todd had waited for her, and when all of his relatives, and her family, had left her studio, they locked up and headed home.

Jessie was silent in the truck on the ride. Todd reached for her hand and laced their fingers together. "What's on your mind?"

"My heart is so full I think it could burst at any moment."

"At least you're feeling positive. My family could be considered overwhelming."

"Oh, I'm totally overwhelmed," she laughed. "But in the most wonderful way." She turned to him. "Todd, they threw me a party, and they invited my mom and sister. Women are usually catty and callous—especially business-women. But these women..."

"They're unique, aren't they?"

Jessie let out a sigh. "I love every one of them. It's like gaining an entire group of sisters. And brothers and cousins," she added. "My whole life was me and my sister. Of course, my brother too, for that short amount of time that we had him. I didn't have what you have."

He gave her hand a squeeze. "Lydia wishes she were here. She sends her love. She's happy for us and she didn't think I'd ever get married," he snorted a laugh.

Jessie eased back in her seat. "We won't even think of getting married until she's home. She needs to be here."

"I agree. But she'll be here soon. I'm not supposed to say anything to anyone, so you didn't hear it from me."

"Then what will you do?" she asked. "Go back to the ranch?"

He shrugged. "I don't know. But everything will fall into place. I think she'll need me for a bit. After that, I guess I'll have some decisions to make. However, I won't make them alone. We're a team now, you and I. I suppose that'll be a bonus that comes with marriage. Someone to help you decide," he joked and she let out a sigh.

"You realize I'll be a business-owning Walker woman."

"A force to be reckoned with, for sure."

And he knew she'd be as successful as the rest of the Walker women.

TODD HELPED Jessie carry all of her gifts into the house. She still couldn't believe in a few hours her new family could throw together something so wonderful.

Every time she thought of how lucky she was, she would tear up.

As she sorted through the gifts, and put the leftovers sent home with her away, Todd stayed out of sight. Perhaps he was too afraid she'd start crying.

"Got a minute?" he called from the living room.

"Yeah, let me put this last bit in the fridge."

She finished putting the extra condiments in the refrigerator's door, then she made sure the extra cake was well wrapped. As she secured the lid on it, she let her finger drag through the icing.

Walking into the living room, she sucked the icing off her

finger, and stopped when she saw Todd on one knee, a ring box in his hand.

"What are you doing?" she asked as she made sure her finger was clean.

"I'm making this a more appropriate proposal."

"You already did that," she said, but her eyes were fixed on the ruby in the box.

"My aunt doesn't think so." He smiled up at her.

Jessie moved toward him, and instinct had her kneeling down in front of him.

"Jessie," he began, "I love you. My aunt gave me this ring to give to you. It was one of my grandmother's. She thought you'd appreciate it."

"Todd, it's beautiful."

"Just like you," he offered as he took the ring from the box. He set the box on the floor and held the ring out. Jessie lifted her hand to him. "I'll buy you any ring you want, but this is yours to pass on to one of our daughters some day."

Now the tears fell, as they had threatened to. "Oh, Todd."

"Will you marry me? Officially?"

This time she only nodded, because she couldn't even speak.

"That makes me as happy as it did last night."

Jessie laughed through the tears as he slid the ring on her finger and she held it up to look at it.

"Your grandmother had good taste," she humored as she took in the exquisite ring.

"She did. And she would have loved you."

Jessie lifted her wet eyes to his. "You think so?"

"I know so."

She wrapped her arms around his neck and pressed a kiss to his lips. She was so incredibly happy she wasn't sure how she was supposed to contain it.

As she eased back, Todd licked his lips.

"Have you been in the frosting?"

Jessie laughed and wiped the tears from her cheeks. "I don't know what you're talking about," she joked as she rose to her feet, holding her hand out in front of her, taking in the sight of the ring on her finger. "I need to call your aunt."

Todd laughed and pulled his phone from his pocket, opening it up to his aunt's number, and handed it to her.

He'd never expected to propose to the woman he loved without first buying her a ring, but when the moment had been right—it was right. When his aunt had dropped off the ring before the party, Todd had to give it a lot of thought. Did he want to give her a hand-me-down ring? No, it wasn't like that. It was an heirloom, and Jessie understood its significance much better than he had.

He could hear her in the other room gushing about the ring and his proposal. He'd lost count of how many times she'd thanked his aunt.

A few minutes later Jessie returned with his phone.

"Lydia texted you while I was talking to your aunt," she said and stood near as he looked at the text.

When he looked up at her, he was sure she'd already seen its contents.

Three days and counting.

CHAPTER 34

Sunday morning Todd pulled his truck into the lot of the *Bridal Mecca* morning and slowed as he realized Phillip was standing next to his patrol car and four other patrol cars were parked around the building. They'd wrapped yellow tape around the pillars that led to the reception hall.

Not worrying about being in a specific parking space, Todd put his truck in the lot, and killed the engine before stepping out.

Phillip walked toward him. "You'll want to make sure you turn over this footage."

"What's going on?"

"You're our latest victim. This time they broke in and hit your liquor supply."

"And you didn't call me?"

Phillip held up a hand to ward off the verbal attack Todd was ready to unleash.

"It's Sunday morning. I knew when you'd be here to open for church. No need to cause you more stress."

Todd wasn't sure if he appreciated the sentiment or not. "How much did they get away with?"

Phillip shrugged. "You'll have to go in and assess. There are a few broken bottles. The bigger mess is what they did to the lock on the storage room. Otherwise, everything seems to be okay."

They began walking toward the entrance. "How is it these loons haven't been caught yet?"

"They're careful. Or careful enough to cover themselves so we can't see them. They don't drive a car, and can easily be lost on video when they run off through buildings or bushes. Honestly, minus the few fires, I'd peg them for some rowdy teenagers just stirring up trouble."

"Great, that makes me feel so much better," Todd bit out the words as they walked into the hall and toward the closet that was used to store the alcohol.

Sure enough, the door had been ripped from its hinges, but the padlock remained securely tightened.

"Looks like we're going to have to rethink good security."

Phillip laughed. "A closed and padlocked door usually deters adequately. They wanted in and they got in. What I don't understand is why your alarm didn't go off."

Todd thought back to the event that had been held Saturday night. It was a wedding, and he'd locked the door around two in the morning.

During the reception, he'd stayed locked in his office getting everything in order for Lydia's return. He wanted everything to be accessible and easy for her to find if she wanted to jump right back into work.

When the guests departed, and the DJ tore down his equipment, Todd had helped him out with his speakers. He took the dolly back inside, and that was when he realized he hadn't even turned on the alarm. All he'd wanted to do was close up and go home to Jessie, knowing he'd be back bright and early the next morning.

"I didn't set the alarm," he admitted and noted the disappointed look on Phillip's face. "It happens."

Todd walked through the doorway to the storage room and

noted that they'd taken all the Jack Daniels, three bottles of vodka, and at least four cases of beer.

"Sounds like if we look hard enough, we'll find someone passed out in a gutter," Phillip joked, apparently trying to lighten the mood.

"I expect you to have this all cleared up in a jiffy then." Todd shook his head and looked around the room.

"I guess they didn't like champagne."

Todd looked at the smashed bottles on the floor and then up onto the shelves. "Shit!"

"This is the expensive stuff?"

"What? No. There was a special bottle though. Damnit. Lydia is going to kill me over that one."

"What's so special about one bottle of champagne?"

Todd shrugged his shoulders. "I have no idea. There was a bottle on the top shelf, behind the others, that she made very clear it wasn't to be served, drank, or removed."

Phillip narrowed his eyes. "A bottle of champagne?"

"Yes." Todd raked his fingers through his hair. "It had some gold label on it. I don't know. I forgot it was up there, but now..." he pointed to the pile on the floor.

Phillip's eyes went wide as he squatted down to look at the pile of broken glass. "Dear God."

"What? Why is it so special?"

He watched as Phillip chewed his bottom lip before he stood. "Not important. Just a bottle of champagne. Not even a good bottle or very expensive." Phillip rubbed his fingers across his forehead. "I'll send in one of my officers for your statement. You'll probably need to call the church and tell them what happened. I suppose they could have service in the parking lot. It's nice enough."

"Sure, I'll call them. Are you okay though?" Todd asked noting that Phillip looked pale.

"Yeah. Yeah, I'm fine. Just have a lot of work to do. I'll let you know if we find anything."

Phillip turned and walked out of the room.

Todd followed. "Do you want the security footage?"

"Right. Yeah, send that over too. Maybe they showed their faces this time."

Phillip walked out of the reception hall and Todd watched him disappear out to the parking lot.

Todd walked back to the closet and knelt down by the pile of glass in the floor. As Phillip had said it was just a bottle of champagne, but something about it had spooked him.

Another officer walked in behind Todd. "We already took pictures and documented all of this. All I need is to get your statement and you're free to clean it all up. I'll never understand why people break into places and make such messes," he said looking at the pile of glass on the floor.

"I'll never understand it either."

CHAPTER 35

*T*odd helped the church move to the parking lot, and he was grateful that they appreciated the sunshine and the opportunity to worship in God's space.

While they held their service outside, Todd finished up his report with the police, turned over the footage of two men kicking in the door and prying the liquor closet door open and off its hinges. At some point, something must have spooked them because they had started for the office door when one of them motioned to the other to get out, and so they did.

Certainly, had they stayed, there would have been more damage.

One thing was for sure. Todd wouldn't call Lydia and tell her what had happened. If his calculations were correct, she should walk through the door at any time. The last thing he wanted was for her to see that champagne bottle broken into shards on the floor. Whatever the reason to keep it safe and hidden, he didn't know. And he wondered why Phillip seemed so stunned to have seen it.

Todd had long ago given up trying to understand the dynamics between Phillip and Lydia. Surely, for the rest of their lives, Phillip would pursue and Lydia would run. And yet, there was a mutual respect that went both ways with both of them.

His phone buzzed in his pocket and he smiled when he noticed Jessie's face on his screen as he pulled it out.

"Hey, beautiful," he greeted as he set the broom he was using against the wall. "Good morning."

"You didn't call me."

"Was I supposed to?"

"The hall was broken into. You should have called me. Are you hurt? Are you in danger?" Her voice was elevated in pitch and volume.

"Those two punks who have been hitting businesses broke into the liquor room. That's all. I'm not in danger. How did you hear about this?"

"Big Finn is at church in the parking lot."

Todd sighed. "Right. I handed him a stack of chairs after he told me he was fit as a fiddle and could handle it. He also promised to sit in one of the chairs, after he set them up, and not to do any more strenuous work," he told her, trying to keep his voice light.

"This isn't a joke."

"I'm not making it one. It's very serious, and I get that."

He heard her let out a long breath. "When are you coming home?"

"I'll probably stay until church is over. We'll have to bring in the chairs, and I need to be very vigilant to set the alarm today."

There was silence on the other end and he wondered if she'd hung up.

Just as Todd was going to ask if she was there, he heard her sniff. "What's wrong?"

"I just got scared. That's all. I wasn't sure what you walked into, and Finn, well, he made it sound much worse."

Todd smiled, making sure that she didn't hear him chuckle. "It's some broken and missing bottles. I have to fix the door and probably the doorjamb to the entrance. I'm okay. They're not out to hurt anyone, they're just causing a little damage."

"They set fire to that salon and to those bushes."

"You're right. They did. Nothing like that will happen. They're starting to get careless. They looked right into the camera at least three times."

"That doesn't calm my nerves," she admitted.

"I'll tell you what. Why don't you get ready, pick up some drive thru breakfast sandwiches, and come be with me? I still have to lock up, and since all of our items are in the parking lot, I will stay till the end."

She hesitated for a moment. "I'll do that. I wanted to do more editing too. Maybe I can get in a few minutes doing that."

"It sounds like our day is planned. I love you," he said before she could say goodbye.

"I love you."

~*~

JESSIE PICKED up Todd's gym bag, and her own, as she left the house. Knowing him, he'd want to make sure everything was where it belonged, and because of the break-in, he'd want to make sure it was all locked up and secure before he left. She didn't blame him for that. She'd seen the text. Lydia was due back at any minute. That didn't mean she'd run right to her office, or even want to see anyone. Since Todd technically still lived in her house, though he hadn't stayed in months, she'd most likely tell him first.

He went to her house daily to check on everything. He tended to her mail, her plants, her housekeeping. Even though he hadn't stayed there, he'd dusted and vacuumed regularly, and had left the dishwasher, and wash machine doors open so they wouldn't mold.

Every weekend, usually after he opened the hall for church, now that spring had arrived, he'd stopped and mowed the small lawn.

Todd took pride in taking care of Lydia, and Jessie wondered how that would go over when she got home. From everything she'd ever heard about Lydia Morgan, she liked to take care of herself. She couldn't help but wonder too if Todd would continue to take care of Lydia, and would Jessie feel jealous over it?

There was no reason for jealousy, and she knew it. And, she wasn't a jealous woman. Then again, she'd never had anything to be jealous over.

Jessie had been in relationships before, but never had they held the promise of marriage.

She looked down at her finger where Todd's grandmother's ring rested. No, there was no reason to be jealous when a man would give a woman his grandmother's heirloom ring.

A smile formed on her lips as she loaded their things into her car.

When her sister had become engaged, Jessie was happy for her. Though not interested in wedding details, she was glad her sister was in love. Never in a million years would she have guessed that before her sister even said, "I do," she, too, would be engaged.

They had set no dates, or even talked about when they'd get married, and Jessie wasn't in any rush. But she thought a winter wedding would be every bit as beautiful as a spring one. Perhaps a destination wedding would be nice.

The thought humored her as she opened the door and slid into her car.

CHAPTER 36

*J*essie dribbled the ball down the court, nudging out the other team, taking an elbow to the side as she skirted around the man covering her. But when she heard Big Finn's cheer from the side of the court when she did a layup at the buzzer, the score didn't matter. Having him there thrilled her and she smiled up at him pumping her fist in the air.

Her father hadn't even cheered for her that loudly while she played growing up—and he'd always been a vocal fan. However, since they had released Finn from the hospital, he'd been right there every week cheering her on.

"You make all the other guys feel bad," she told Finn as she hugged him after she shook hands with the members of the other team.

"Why?"

"You're here for me. They think you should cheer them on too."

Finn lifted a brow. "None of them are as adorable as you are."

That made her laugh as Todd walked up to them.

"Is this guy giving you a hard time?" he joked, looking up at the giant of a man standing next to him.

"You know. Says he wants to take me out for a beer," she said, and Finn laughed.

"I owe you beer for the rest of your life. Without me, I wouldn't be cheering you on."

"Eh, I fell to the ground faster than the rest to get to you. They all would have taken care of you. I don't doubt it for a minute."

Finn smiled and nodded, and Jessie knew he understood that was the truth. "I'll head out then. But I'll have a beer ready for you when you get there."

"We'll be right behind you."

Jessie and Todd watched Finn walk out the door. "He looks good," Todd said.

"He does. I guess you just never know when things will happen."

Todd nodded slowly. "You're right."

"I'm going to be ten minutes getting a shower. I'll meet you over at the bar."

She closed her eyes as Todd leaned in and kissed her gently on the cheek. "Do you want a plate of wings? Or should I order a pizza?"

"I'm hungry enough for both, but you choose one and I'll be happy."

"I'm going to drive by Lydia's and just make sure everything looks okay."

She nodded as she lifted her bag up over her shoulder and headed toward the locker room.

~*~

TODD HAD CLEARED out all his belongings from Lydia's house the day before. And while he was sitting at the YMCA he'd received the text *I am home*.

There was no reason for him to keep the news from Jessie, but Lydia had asked that no one know she was coming home—not yet. He would keep that promise.

It would be no time at all before everyone knew, and he assumed Phillip would be the first. He could probably sense her in the state.

The thought made him chuckle. He'd be that way with Jessie. There was a sensation when she was near, or on her way home, or even just thinking of him. That was true love.

As Todd drove down Lydia's street, he could see the glow of her living room light. Her neighbors would be accustomed to seeing it. He'd set it up on a timer so that the house didn't appear to be empty when he'd started staying at Jessie's. But he knew the truth behind the light tonight.

There was a nervous surge that zipped through him as he parked in front of her house. He'd seen Lydia during their chats and talked to her nearly every day for the year she was gone. But there was something to knowing she was behind that door that had his nerves on fire.

As he parked and killed the engine, he wished he'd stopped for flowers or something. Then again, that might just piss her off.

Yeah, this visit would do that too, but he couldn't help it. She needed to know he was glad she was home. He'd have brought his whole family if he knew it would be a welcomed gesture.

Todd stepped out of the truck and started for the door when it opened. "I sent you that text an hour ago. I was certain you'd have a welcome party for me by now," she joked, and it lit into her eyes.

At that moment the nerves turned into emotion and he thought he might cry at the sight of her.

"And you would have kicked my ass."

"Oh, boy, wouldn't I have?"

She stepped out onto the porch and he enveloped her in his arms. Until that moment he'd forgotten just how little she was.

181

Her five-foot-three was tiny when he scooped her up and just held her.

There was a moment he thought she'd started to cry, but this was Lydia. That had been sucked up and hidden by the time he set her back on her feet.

Her moist eyes looked up at him. "I've missed you. I've missed all of you." She turned and opened the door. "Come in for a minute."

Todd followed her into the house which now felt different with her presence in it. He laughed when he noticed she'd moved the living room furniture around.

"I needed it to be different," she admitted as she closed the door. "I think I'll put it on the market and buy a new house. I didn't think being back in here would be a big deal, but I think it will be."

"Jessie and I are working with a real estate agent I think you'd like."

The corners of her mouth turned up into a smile. "I can't believe you're getting married and buying a house. What has the world come to? The Walker men will all be married."

"Doesn't even seem possible."

"I pegged you long ago to be in the middle of the herd, not the last one."

He wasn't sure how to take that, but it made him laugh. "And who did you peg to be last?"

"Originally, Eric. Who'd have thought he'd be the first? That man had a stick up his ass for so long."

He thought of the feud between her family and his, and it had long ago snowballed when Eric's mother and his uncle had gotten involved, and Eric was the product of that. And now, his own sister was married to Lydia's brother. It was interesting how one generation could change everything.

Lydia walked back to the kitchen and Todd followed.

"You know, seriously, I thought Jake would never get married.

And I didn't expect he'd fall in love with the woman who caused him to lose races."

"Now, that one makes more sense," Todd said. "Though, I think deep inside the reason he and Missy hated each other was because of the attraction."

He saw her flinch, and he wondered what he'd stumbled on.

Lydia picked up a cup of tea that had been steeping on the counter "Do you have time for some dinner? Someone stocked my fridge."

Todd chuckled. "I'm headed to the bar with Jessie and her team. Big Finn owes her a beer or twelve."

"She saved his life I hear."

"I think in many ways." At that moment he realized that. "You're welcome to come."

Lydia smiled from behind her mug as she took a sip of her tea. "Not yet. I won't hide forever, but not yet."

"I understand. Everyone will know you're here. They'll feel you."

"I'm sure Phillip already knows. Does he just patrol this street now?"

Todd grinned down at her. "He misses you. Maybe throw him a bone for the first week."

"I'm done hating, Todd. It takes too much effort. I'm ready to get back to work and get on with my life. I have to the tools to deal with everything that comes up, and I'm going to handle it."

"I'm proud of you. You have no idea how proud."

"I'm proud of me too." She set the mug on the counter and moved in to hug him again. "Thank you for everything."

"It is my pleasure. I'm here for you always. You're like another sister to me."

"And family, no matter the kind, is the most important thing."

odd had taken longer than he'd meant to, but there was no way he could drive by Lydia's without stopping.

Jessie's car was in the parking lot when he pulled up to the bar, and a wave of guilt washed over him. He hadn't done anything wrong, but not telling her that Lydia was home suddenly ate at him.

When he walked into the bar, he spotted her at a tall bar table with Finn and four other men. They each had a beer in front of them, and a large platter of nachos between them. Finn was telling a story, and before he reached them, they all burst into laughter.

Her eyes sparkled when she laughed and the guilt twisted in his belly.

"Hey, sexy," she said as he walked up next to her and took the kiss she offered. "I beat you."

Her voice was light an airy, and there wasn't a hint of disappointment in it.

"Just needed to check on things."

Finn waved the waitress down and ordered Todd a beer.

"How's the hall? Can't believe someone would break into it. What's going on in this town?"

Todd shrugged as the waitress returned with his beer. "I think it's just some young punks trying to see what they can get away with."

"They're ruining businesses. And that's the livelihoods of the people around here."

"I think their reign of terror is almost over. The footage I got of them is clear. Someone will recognize them and come forward."

"That had to cost Lydia a pretty penny though."

Todd thought of what was taken, and the cost was negligible, as was the cost to fix the door. But he still wondered about the sentimental cost of the bottle that broke.

Jessie sat with her teammates and her fiancé and wondered if the dynamic would soon change. Would meeting up at the bar on Sunday nights after their game still be a thing when she got married? Then again, why would it change? It hadn't changed since she'd gotten involved with Todd, he'd just become a part of it.

The thought filled her with warmth—he'd just become a part of it. He'd settled into her world, just as she'd settled into his. There was no doubt that he'd sit and have a drink with Finn, just as she spent time in Pearl's store having wine and cheese platters with his family.

Jessie thought she could almost cry. She loved him so much, and he was all hers.

But as she watched him talk to the other men, she could see something behind his eyes. There was worry.

Was it about the *Bridal Mecca* and the break-in? Or was it because of Lydia and her homecoming?

Jessie knew that Lydia should have arrived. She'd seen the text the other night. But he hadn't said anything, nor would he, she assumed. Lydia would need to integrate herself back into everything. She'd been gone nearly a year.

One by one the men finished their beers, ate their nachos, and headed home. Soon, Finn did the same, and Todd and Jessie moved to the table where they'd first got to know each other.

"I'm glad Finn is doing so well," Todd said after they had ordered wings.

"It'll be a while before he's on the court again, if he gets back. But, yeah, I'm glad too." She watched him take a thoughtful sip of his beer. "How is she?" It was time to ask.

Todd lifted his eyes to her and for the first time she couldn't read them and know what he was thinking. "She's fine." He let out a breath. "How did you know?"

"I knew she was coming, remember? I just didn't know when for sure."

He nodded and reached for her hand. "She looks good. She's feisty as ever, but I think she's anxious. Reintegrating herself will be a process, but she says she has the tools to manage it."

"Were you going to tell me you saw her?" Jessie asked and felt the stirring of jealousy kick up in her belly.

"I didn't mean to upset you by…"

"You didn't," she admitted. "I've been wondering when this would kick in and I guess it's here."

"What's that?"

"Jealousy over Lydia."

Todd furrowed his brows. "You're jealous over Lydia?"

"I said I knew I would be."

"I'm not understanding the difference."

She noticed his grip on her hand grew tighter. "I've never been around Lydia, yet everything revolves around her. Where I work. Where you lived. The job you do. And now, her homecoming. You have to understand that I don't know your feelings for her when she's here in person."

"You'd better damn well know that they're the same as when she's gone. She's like a sister to me and you're the woman I'm going to marry." His voice was rising along with the noise in the bar.

"Todd, I don't want to upset you—"

"You did. I can't believe you're jealous." He pulled back his hand and the jealous swirl in her belly intensified.

"I think I deserve some time to figure out how this makes me feel."

"At what cost?"

"None. Some time. I don't know. You have no right to be mad at me."

"You're mad at me," he reminded her.

"For not telling me you went to see her."

Todd drew in a breath before taking a long drink from his beer. "She texted me she was home during your game. She doesn't want anyone to know she's here yet."

"I get it," she admitted, sipping her beer. And she did get it, so why were they arguing? "This is going to happen again when I see her, meet her, see you with her," she offered, hoping that he'd understand she needed to process what was going on.

"I love you."

"I love you too. There is no doubt there."

"And since you've walked through my *daddy issues*," he said using air quotes with his fingers, "you deserve to have Lydia issues."

There was a tinge of humor in his eyes now. "So we both understand. I get to process this. We still love each other, and this changes nothing."

"The only thing it changes is we live together now. I'm not driving out to my old place, which has a lease option by the way, and I can't run to Lydia's to stay. When you're mad at me and you lock me out of the bedroom now, I sleep on the couch—or you do. We're in this—together."

"I don't want it any other way. And I want to get married in December," she blurted out the thought she'd had earlier.

The anger that had masked his face dissolved, and a smile formed on his lips. "The girls will be happy to have a date finally."

"Have they been asking you about that?"

"Of course. Pearl wants to help you with a dress. Bethany wants to know your colors. Gia wants to make sure she's in town and not in Italy buying things for her store. The list goes on."

And this, she thought was what it was all about. They could have insecurities and arguments, but they would talk them through and move on. Their marriage would be solid. There was no doubt about it.

CHAPTER 38

They'd gone another round over Lydia when they'd returned home, though Jessie hadn't meant to. Jealousy was an ugly beast, and she knew it, but she couldn't help it.

Todd had taken his pillow to the couch, just as he said he would, but she'd gone to him and with his hand in hers, she'd led him back to the bedroom where they slept in one another's arms.

The lack of sleep showed in her eyes when she studied them in the mirror the next morning before work.

An hour later, she was in her studio, watching Pearl walk through the door with two coffees. And this, she knew, was also how things would work. There would always be a third party.

"I know you don't want me involved, but I am," she said to announce herself as she walked through the door and closed it with her hip. "I meddle and I listen."

Pearl smiled as she handed Jessie one of the white paper cups.

"Thank you," Jessie said taking the cup and nodding toward the chairs at the front of the studio for them to sit down.

Pearl, looking as elegant as she did every day, sat in the chair near the portrait of her family and smiled up at it. "You certainly created a masterpiece with that one."

"Thank you. I'll be hard-pressed to enjoy my wedding photos as much, I suppose. I have grand ideas of what I want. I just have to find the right photographer."

Pearl crossed her legs and held her coffee cup balanced on her knee. "December, I hear?"

"I think so."

"I like December weddings. So elegant."

"But you're not here to talk about my December wedding, are you?"

A smile formed on Pearl's lips as she lifted her coffee and took a sip, leaving a trace of lipstick on the lid. "He's upset."

"And he should be. I know that," Jessie admitted. "I take blame for all of this."

"Don't. It's a human reaction. However, as Lydia's sister-in-law, and Todd's sister, I can tell you that their relationship is equal to the one I have with him. And if Lydia thought, for a minute, that she'd driven some kind of wedge between the two of you, she'd pack up and go back to Hawaii."

Jessie eased in her seat. "Go back. So you know that…"

"That she's here? Yeah, I know."

"How?"

"I'm married to her brother."

Jessie nearly laughed. "Right."

"Anyway, I just want to say, cut Todd some slack. He's going to have to spend a lot of time with her as she starts to figure out her life here. We're all going to coddle her a little, because, damn, what she went through wasn't pretty, or easy. I wouldn't wish that on anyone."

And though Pearl hadn't meant to, she made Jessie feel small with her words.

"I'll reel it in. I don't want anyone upset. Not Todd. Not Lydia. Not you."

"Not you either," Pearl said as she stood and Jessie followed. "If you feel jealous, come see me. I'm a woman. I get it. I'm a sister. I'm a best friend. I'm all of those things for you. You're not alone."

Tears stung Jessie's throat. "I appreciate that."

Pearl moved in and hugged Jessie before walking toward the door. "Your sister is coming in for a fitting today. Why don't I order in lunch and you come by too?"

Jessie thought of her schedule. "I have a cake smash at two."

"Plenty of time. She'll be there at ten-thirty."

"I'll come over."

Pearl gave Jessie a little wave as she let herself out of the studio just as the man delivering UPS let himself in.

"Oh, fantastic," Jessie said as she saw the writing on the side of the box. "Thank you."

The man held out his tablet and Jessie signed for the new light that she'd ordered.

As the man left, she studied the box. Luckily, she'd have time to set it up and mess with it before her sister arrived at Pearl's store. Jessie loved that business was good enough she could buy new equipment to make her portraits even better masterpieces, as Pearl had said.

~*~

Lydia had called, but she hadn't yet made her way to the reception hall. And as far as Todd knew, he, his sister, and Lydia's brother were the only people that knew she was back in town. Of course, Jessie did too, and hadn't that opened a can of worms?

Todd checked in the new liquor order, and watched the men who would fix the door that had been ripped off its hinges, carry in their tools. By the end of the day, there would be no signs that someone had broken in.

Phillip walked through the reception hall and straight to Todd's office.

"We got one of them," he boasted, and Todd thought perhaps the man might smile, though he kept his face serious. "There are four guys who have been busting up places, we thought there were only two, and he's giving us names. I have officers picking up two of the men right now."

"And the last guy?"

"We'll get him, but we haven't found him yet. I would guess he realizes his alliances aren't very strong."

Todd nodded. "I'm glad to have this over."

"It'll be over when that last guy is in my custody." Phillip looked toward the men who were fixing the door. "Everything under control here?"

"Back on schedule," Todd offered.

"She hasn't come in yet?"

Todd narrowed his eyes on Phillip. "Who?"

"Don't play stupid, even if she wants you to. I know she's home. Call it a sixth sense. I know when she's within a hundred-mile radius."

"No, she hasn't been in. And she doesn't want anyone to know she's here yet."

Phillip nodded. "I figured. She'll take her time and slowly integrate back in. I know how she thinks. But this will be the first place she comes."

"I assume so. Nice and tidy. She can integrate back and hide in her office."

Phillip chuckled, and Todd took that as a good sign that the man might ease up a bit. "You're right. I'll let you know when we get that last guy in custody."

"Thanks."

Phillip turned to walk out of the office, then stopped and turned back to Todd. "Tell her I'm thinking about her, and I'm glad she's home. I know for a fact, I'll be the last person to see her, and that's okay. I'm just glad she's home."

"I'll let her know," Todd promised and watched as Phillip Smythe walked out of the reception hall, his shoulders hunched, and his heart still obviously broken.

CHAPTER 39

There was a dress displayed in Pearl's store that caught Jessie's eye. She didn't do more than look at it from across the room as her sister changed into her dress. Until her sister walked down that aisle in June, Jessie wouldn't plan a single thing.

But, perhaps, she would casually touch the dress on her way out of Pearl's store.

"Your father still has his tuxedo from when we got married," her mother's voice snapped Jessie from looking at the dress. "I think it's a terrible idea for him to wear it, but he wants to use it to save money. I can't even imagine it would fit," her mother said with a laugh.

"And this is something that's hanging in his closet?"

"In the basement."

"So make it disappear. Has he looked at it?"

Her mother's brows drew together. "No. He just knows that's where it is."

"Easily removable."

Jessie's mother smiled at her and gave Jessie's hand a pat. "Good idea. I suppose we'll be in here soon for you too."

"We'll make plans when Carlie's wedding is over. I don't want to step on any toes. No need to."

"Have you and Todd found a house yet?"

"Not yet. Things have been busy. But maybe in the next few weeks we can look more seriously," she said, knowing that once Lydia went back to work, that would open up Todd's schedule.

Carlie emerged from the dressing room, and both women stood in response to the awe of seeing her in the dress.

Their mother clasped her hands and pressed them to her lips. "Oh, sweetheart, don't you look beautiful?"

"Thanks, Mama." Carlie spun in front of the three-way mirror. "It's so close. I can't believe it's almost here."

Pearl stood to the side and watched as the seamstress moved in and began to pin the fabric. "That dress is perfect, Carlie. You should have your sister do a bridal sitting for you. We can have Audrey do your hair, and Bethany set up some flowers. We could use the photos in all the stores."

Jessie turned her attention to Pearl who smiled at her. "That would be fun."

Carlie turned to face them. Tears pooled in her eyes. "A sitting with just me in my dress?"

Pearl nodded. "The pictures would be phenomenal."

Carlie looked at Jessie. "What do you think?"

"I think it's a fantastic idea."

Carlie looked back in the mirror. "It would be nice to have one more opportunity to wear this and get all fancied up. Let's do it."

The seamstress finished her pinning and took some notes before Carlie slipped out of the dress. Jessie kissed her mother and sister goodbye as they left the store, carried the wine glasses they had used to the back room, and started out of the bridal shop after giving Sunshine a wave goodbye.

"Hold on," Pearl said before she made it to the door. "Come try it on."

Jessie turned slowly. "Try what on?"

"The dress you've been ogling without actually going up to see it so you didn't hurt your sister's feelings."

Jessie laughed. "It's particularly spooky how you can read people."

"It's a gift," she humored as she held out her hand as if to direct Jessie back to the room. "I set it in room three. Go try it on."

Warmth moved into Jessie's cheeks and she smiled at her future sister-in-law as she passed her and hurried toward the dressing room.

It was exactly as Jessie had hoped. When she looked at herself in the mirror in the tiny little room, she thought she might cry. There had never been a day when she thought she'd wanted all the frilly things that went with a wedding, but she did.

"Are you coming out?" Pearl called from the other room.

When Jessie opened the door, she immediately noticed Bethany and Audrey seated on the couch.

Audrey tapped her fingers together in a silent applause. "We had to come see what our newest sister would be wearing," she said, and it squeezed at Jessie's heart.

"It's the most exquisite thing I've ever seen," Jessie said as she spun in front of the mirror. "And it fits. Nothing in my life ever fits," she laughed and turned to the women who watched her.

Pearl moved to her and adjusted the fabric. "I don't get too many tall brides, but when I got this dress in, I knew it would flatter you."

"You hung this up so I would see it?"

Pearl shrugged. "It just seemed right."

These women were the women who she would turn to now. They would be her sisters, just as Audrey had said. She would share with them as much as she shared with her sister.

Falling in love with Todd had just been one of the steps in changing her life, she realized. She wasn't just marrying him; she was marrying an entire family. Soon she would have sisters, a brother, and cousins that a year ago she didn't know. Was there a luckier woman in the world than her? She already had a perfect family, and now she was getting another.

She thought for a moment about how Todd could get so worked up over his parents, but she saw what he really had. His family was incredible. Jessie was honored that she'd soon carry the Walker name.

CHAPTER 40

*E*ven Monday evenings deserved champagne with a simple dinner of spaghetti and garlic bread.

Todd leaned against the doorjamb, and she gazed at him as she mixed the sauce into the pasta.

"You could be helpful and carry some of this to the table," she offered as he stood there smiling at him.

"You're almost glowing. What's got you all giddy?" he asked as he moved into the kitchen and pressed a kiss to her cheek before taking the bowl of salad to the table.

"I found my dress," she said as she lifted the pasta bowl and followed him.

"You mean my sister found something that was perfect for you?"

Jessie let out a sigh. "Yes. How did you know that?"

"I told you. She has a way about reading people."

Jessie sat down at the table and Todd followed. "I won't plan anything until my sister's wedding is over. I don't want to step on her toes."

Todd lifted salad from the bowl with the tongs and set it on her plate and then did the same for his. "That's understandable.

She's had a few sisters go rounds in her store. I mean fists and all."

Jessie looked up from serving the pasta and stared at him. "Are you kidding?"

He shook his head. "Nope. You wouldn't believe how brutal bridal dress sales could get."

She laughed as she picked up her napkin and set it in her lap. "I get a pushy mom once in a while. You know, they know how to seat their baby for a photo better than I do."

"I suppose every profession has that. Well," he gave a thoughtful look as he picked up his fork, "I can't say I ever had that on the ranch. My uncle, though he might not always agree with me, would let me do things my way when it suited me."

"And how did that work out?"

Now he laughed too. "I often fixed it to do it his way, because he was right."

~*~

Todd tossed and turned all night. There was something that kept creeping into his dreams that would make him wake up, check the time, and roll back over.

Around one, he walked to the kitchen, filled a glass of water, and drank it down. The air seemed unsettled. Maybe they were going to get a storm. Maybe he'd forgotten to turn off a light at the hall. Maybe Jessie's excitement over the dress had transferred to him. But it didn't feel like excitement—this troubling feeling that was keeping him up.

When he'd finished his water, he headed back to bed. Jessie rolled in her sleep and he took a moment to appreciate the look of her at peace.

Leaning in, he pressed a kiss gently to her head, and in sleep, she sighed.

For thinking he'd never love someone in his life, it sure was a glorious feeling to have wandered into it. He was grateful that Carlie had chosen the reception hall and had dragged her sister with her.

Settling into bed, he draped an arm over Jessie and eased himself against her. His eyelids grew heavy and sleep began to take back over.

When his phone rang at three o'clock, both he and Jessie sat straight up in bed. Todd's heart raced from the abrupt pull from sleep, as well as knowing that any call at three in the morning wasn't a good thing.

Reaching for his phone on the nightstand, he blinked his eyes to read that it was Lydia calling.

His feet were on the ground before he even connected the call.

"What's wrong?" he started as he pulled the pair of pants from the hamper and began tugging them on. "Are you okay? Where are you?"

"Todd, shut the hell up," she scolded on the other end. "I'm with Phillip. We're at the *Bridal Mecca*. It's on fire."

Surely his heart had stopped. Had he really heard her right?

Todd turned, the phone still pressed to his ear, and stared at Jessie who was perched on her knees on the bed.

"We're on our way," he said before he disconnected the call.

Jessie moved off the bed and to him. "What's wrong? What happened to her? Is she okay?"

He lifted his eyes to meet hers in the dark. "The *Bridal Mecca* is on fire."

CHAPTER 41

*J*essie had taken his keys right from his hand and hurried to his truck. She jumped in behind the wheel, and he hadn't even argued.

She'd seen this kind of look before. Her father had worn that same mask when her brother died. Sure, it was different—a human life versus a building—but she'd seen it.

When they arrived, Jessie parked the truck down Main Street since she couldn't get any closer because they had blocked the street off. The flames kissed the sky, and she realized that it engulfed the entire building.

Todd had bolted from the truck the moment she stopped. She watched as he ran toward the building, only to be stopped by police.

Jessie sat there, in the truck, unable to breathe.

It was burning in front of her. Everything she'd been working for was engulfed in flames.

She watched as Todd wrapped his arm around a small figure and pulled them close to him. Lydia, no doubt. The long, lanky build of Phillip Smythe stood next to her, though his identity was masked in a glowing shadow.

Tears began to roll down Jessie's cheeks as she watched the flames grow.

Car after car piled in behind her, and she watched as Pearl and Tyson, Audrey and Gregory, Gia and Dane, Ella and Gerald, Nichole and Ben, and Bethany and Kent all hurried toward Lydia and Todd.

There was a line of them now watching as flames consumed what they'd worked for.

Jessie sucked in as much breath as she could, but her head was feeling light and tears skewed her vision. This was a death like no other. This was a death of dreams and hard work. She wasn't sure she could even face it.

When Todd pulled open the door to the truck, she screamed. She hadn't even seen him come toward her.

"Hey, hey," he eased her from the seat and wrapped his arms around her. "Calm down."

"Oh, Todd. This is horrible."

"It's a building."

"No, no," she stammered through her tears. "It's so much more than that. It's dreams and family. Oh, God! All of their dreams are gone. All of mine…"

She fell against his chest and let him hold her.

"You should be with all of them," he said, and she shook her head, her face buried against his chest.

"I don't belong there."

Todd eased her back. "You belong there as much as any of them. You're part of them. You're in the same boat. This sucks. This is watching what you worked so hard for literally go up in flames. And I have no doubt that by six o'clock, every one of you will have a plan how to go on."

Jessie's eyes burned as the wind shifted smoke in their direction.

Taking Todd's hand, she let him lead her toward the line of Walker women who watched their businesses swept up in flame.

Pearl took hold of her hand and gave it a squeeze. "It's a setback. A minor blip on the radar," she said through tears that choked her voice. "This isn't going to stop us."

There was an arm around each of the women, including Phillip's around Lydia. When the flames burst through the front of Jessie's studio, she felt her knees go weak, and Todd's arms held her up.

Not one single store front didn't have flames in it. Not one single store front would be salvageable. Not one single one of them would have anything left, Jessie thought as the flames went higher.

Susan and Eric, and Russell and Chelsea emerged from the darkness and joined arms with the others. The screeching of tires behind them had them all turning to see Missy and Jake walking toward them all. Each and every Walker had come. She would assume Todd's aunt and uncle were with children so they could all stand united as they watched the flames dismantle what they'd built.

They stood there for hours as the fire engulfed, then the firefighters eventually prevailed. As the sun began to rise in the smoke-filled sky, they all remained, taking in the sight of the charred building that remained before them.

Lydia still hooked under Phillip's arm, walked toward them.

"I've been standing here for hours, and I didn't even introduce myself," she said to Jessie as she held out her hand. "Lydia Morgan."

Jessie's words stuck in her throat as she reached out and shook Lydia's hand. "Jessie."

"Looks like we have a lot of work ahead of us."

"I'm so sorry for all of this. How horrible to come back to this."

Lydia shrugged. "It sucks. It sucks big time. But if I let every setback hold me down, I'd be dead."

Pearl moved in toward them, wrapping her arm around Lydia

and kissing her on the head. "The fire chief says it'll be hours before they're done here, and it could be days before we can get in and see the damage. We're all going to gather our families and head out to the ranch. Glenda is setting up breakfast and we're all going to sit down, defuse, and plan." She turned her attention fully to Lydia. "Are you up for this?"

"No better time to reintegrate than now."

Pearl leaned in and kissed Todd on the cheek. "We'll meet you out there." She turned and kissed Jessie on the cheek as well. "This doesn't stop Walker women. You're one of us, and we will rebuild."

As each couple turned and walked away, Jessie stood holding Todd's hand in hers. "How do you rebuild after this? This is devastating. My heart hurts so much I think I could fall to the ground."

"Then do. Fall. Cry. Get pissed. What happens tomorrow?"

She turned to him and stared at him through burning eyes. "I don't know."

"You do it again until you don't fall, or cry, or get pissed. Not one of them is going to let this ruin them. I suspect it won't ruin you either."

"I don't have as much invested in it as they do. This was years of their lives."

"And they'll make it work for them. Look at them all leaving to figure this out. We have weddings that are happening this weekend. I will guarantee by tomorrow, Pearl will have dresses replaced and Lydia will have them a venue."

"What about you?"

"I'll be right there to make sure everything falls into place."

Jessie looked back at the building, now bathed in sunlight, its embers still popping and its face nothing but burned walls.

She wasn't sure it was possible to come back from this. She wasn't sure she wanted to. It hurt in her chest to even think about moving on. How was it these women thought they could talk through this and come out better? Her optimism clearly sucked. She just wanted to go home and hide under the covers.

Todd took her arm and began walking her toward the truck.

He helped her inside, closed the door, and walked around to climb in behind the steering wheel. The engine roared as he started the big truck and pulled away.

"I hope Lydia's ready for all of this. What a sucky thing to happen to her." Todd's words sliced right through the heart that had already been broken that night. But how could she argue? Jessie realized that the jealousy she'd been fighting off now pulsed through her and mingled with her sadness.

As they drove out toward the ranch, the sun rose higher over the horizon. Jessie watched the scenery out the window and fought to push down all the resentment she had. They all wanted to rebuild, but at the moment, she just wanted to run. She wasn't Walker-worthy.

CHAPTER 42

The house at Walker Ranch had grown loud and full of people. All ten of the Walker children, their spouses, and their families filled Glenda Walker's kitchen.

Jessie sat in a chair, just beyond the enormous dining room table, listening to the well-organized thoughts of Lydia and Pearl. Each of them had a legal pad in front of them filled with lists of things that each of them would need to think of immediately, short-term, and long-term.

Glenda fussed over every tired person in the room, including Jessie, which hadn't comforted her, but made her uncomfortable.

"We have to start with the wedding this weekend," Pearl said. "She is in possession of her dress. She picked it up yesterday morning."

Susan, with her own legal pad, leaned in. "I have her menu. I'm on track."

Lydia nodded. "We just need a venue." She tapped her pen to her chin. "I have a text in to my mother to see where she can help us."

What Jessie had learned was that Lydia's entrepreneurship

came naturally. Her mother, too, was business-minded and had her hand in multiple businesses around town.

Pearl lifted a mug of coffee to her lips. "I'll put in a call to the bride around eight o'clock."

Lydia made a note and exchanged looks with Todd. "I'll need you to walk me through the bookings at each venue. We can do that tomorrow."

He nodded and made a note in his cellphone.

Within three hours, the family had solidified plans for the next two weeks. Lydia's mother was able to offer them space in one of her venues. Lydia, Todd, and Bethany had made plans to reconvene in two days to plan out the rest of the contracted bookings.

Audrey walked back into the room, her phone in her hand. "I've put in calls to all the insurance companies on the list. Everyone should expect to get calls back shortly."

Pearl nodded and made a mark on her list.

Audrey pushed her fingers through her hair and sat back in her chair. "I've talked to four local salons and they'll house my stylists until we're back up."

Ella walked from the kitchen with a fresh cup of coffee. "I'm going to rent an office in one of those open work spaces."

Gia finished typing on her phone and then set it down. "I have a text into a real estate friend. As soon as we can work out a short-term lease somewhere, I will reassemble my inventory. We have a trip planned to Italy in July. Maybe insurance will process by then."

Tyson walked behind his sister and rested a hand on her shoulder. "Phillip says the fire investigator is in there now. We should have some word on the fire soon."

Lifting her mug to her lips, Lydia looked around the room. "I think we need to go home and get some sleep. We made some good progress."

. . .

~*~

THE DRIVE HOME had been quiet. Todd's head was filled with lists that had items that needed to be checked off.

He honestly couldn't decide if the fire was a horrific event for Lydia to process, or was it exactly what she needed to reincorporate herself back into the daily life she was always part of.

Shifting a glance at Jessie, who watched the scenery out the window, he realized he had to be sensitive to her loss too. She'd only just started her entrepreneurial journey, and now it was all gone. Her portraits, her equipment, her props were all in that pile of rubble to sort out.

Todd reached for her hand and laced their fingers together, but her gaze did not shift from the window.

"What are you thinking?" he asked as the dirt road gave to pavement.

She shifted in her seat to face him. "That I should go get a job."

"Why would you do that? You have a solid business."

"That's crap, and you know it." Her voice shook. "I have a generous business because of your family. We were neighbors with a like mind in a business model. They sent me everything they could, rarely could I reciprocate."

He hadn't expected her attitude about her business. In fact, he figured that she would be just the opposite, just like his family that was ready to rebuild even before the embers cooled.

"I don't think they see it that way," he assured her.

"You don't know what they think."

"And neither do you," he said not wanting to trump his family loyalty over his loyalty to her, but he couldn't help but shut down her thinking. "Those women consider you one of them. They are ready to rebuild, and that includes you."

She turned her gaze back out the window. Obviously she wasn't in the same mindset as the others—not yet. Todd realized she needed time to process what was going on. He could give her that, but he didn't want her to give up.

As they drove through town, her cellphone rang, and her mother's voice could be heard on the other end. Todd listened as Jessie gave her account of the morning, and when she began to cry, he gave her hand a squeeze.

Exhaustion was taking over, and he could see it darken her eyes. Perhaps he could convince her to lie down when they got home. He'd make her some tea and join her for a few hours of rest.

He wasn't sure how rebuilding the empire they had all made would take shape, but he knew that they would be back—and even better. Lydia and Pearl would rebuild, there was no doubt about that.

Time would convince Jessie of that, he was sure. For now, all he could do was help her through her loss, remembering to be mindful of her misguided feelings toward Lydia.

CHAPTER 43

*J*essie had decided on a hot bath, locking the bathroom door so she would have no interruptions. Setting her music to Adele, she put in her headphones and closed her eyes.

The aromatic scents calmed her as the bubbles rose to her neck.

There was a lot to think about, and she just needed the peace for a bit to wrap her head around what had happened, and where it would lead her.

She'd given full credit for her business to the Walker women, but that wasn't true. They'd sent her business, but it had been her skill, and a keen eye, that had kept them, sold them, and had them coming back.

The last thing she wanted to do was give up on her dream, but when she talked to Todd, she couldn't convince herself that everything would be okay.

It would take the better part of the year to rebuild the *Bridal Mecca*, if that was in fact what Pearl and Lydia did. No doubt she could find a place to put her studio until they rebuilt. As the other women rebuilt their businesses in other locations, surely they would continue to send business her way. Things wouldn't be different forever—just for a while.

As the water began to cool, Jessie pulled her headphones from her ears and dipped her head back into the water, letting the silence sooth her. She owed Todd an apology.

Emerging from the water, she wiped the water from her eyes. A few minutes later she wrapped a towel around her wet hair and tied her plush robe around her body.

She could smell coffee and hear voices as she turned the corner to the kitchen. There was some surprise to see Todd sitting at the table with Officer Smythe.

Both men stood.

"I didn't realize we had company," she said, suddenly very aware of her appearance.

"Phillip had some news about the fire."

Now it didn't matter what she wore. She wanted to know what he had found out. The men sat back down and watched her.

Jessie poured herself a cup of coffee and leaned against the counter. "What did you find out?"

Phillip took a sip of his coffee then pushed the mug away. "Maybe I should let you tell her," he said to Todd.

Todd nodded and Phillip stood from the table. "I'll be back when I have any more news." He picked up his hat and let himself out of the house.

Jessie waited until she heard the front door close, then took the seat he had occupied.

"It wasn't an accident, was it?"

Todd sat down and rested his arms on the table, his mug held between his hands.

"They have reason to believe that the guy, whom they haven't caught yet, was breaking into the building again."

"Thug. Why do this? They haven't even been taking anything. So why break in and set a fire?" Her anger began to rise. "They broke in and burned the damn building down."

Her anger had her standing up and pacing the kitchen.

"Well," he began as he stood up, "they think the guy broke in, but didn't set the fire intentionally."

"Then what the hell happened? We lost everything, business-wise. All of us did. So what happened if it wasn't intentional?"

He moved to her. "They broke into your studio. There is evidence that they pried open the back door. Your computer was in the parking lot."

She held her breath. The bastard had violated her area, and that wasn't settling well.

Todd reached for her hand. "At some point, they knocked over your new light, and it sparked the fire."

She went light-headed, and Todd grabbed her arms to hold her up. Moving to lean against the counter, she lifted her eyes to meet his.

"The fire started in my studio?"

He nodded. "Yes."

Jessie lifted her fingers to her lips. "This was all my fault."

Shaking his head, he lifted her chin with his finger. "It's not your fault. How can you even think that?"

"It was my equipment."

"It was the idiot that broke into steal your things. This has nothing to do with you—I mean you didn't cause this."

"I cost them all their businesses."

"Jess, no. You cannot think like that."

"You do not understand how horrible I feel." She broke from his grasp and hurried down the hall to the bedroom, slamming the door behind her.

She ripped through her drawers and pulled out clothes, not even caring what they were. Dropping her towel and robe on the floor, she pulled on the clothes as Todd knocked on the door.

"Jessie, let's talk."

"Leave me alone," she shouted as she pulled on her shoes and then opened the door. "Just leave me alone."

She passed by him, grabbing her purse and sunglasses off the counter, and pushing the wet strands of hair from her face.

"Where are you going?"

"Away. Just leave me alone. And I promise I will leave you and your family alone."

Now he moved to her more quickly as she made it to the front door. "What are you talking about? You most certainly won't leave me or my family. You are my family. Jessie, this isn't your fault. Come back in and let's talk."

But it was her fault. The pain in her heart told her she was to blame for the loss of every business in that building. How could they ever forgive her for what had happened to them?

Jessie closed her eyes and drew in a breath before pulling from Todd and hurrying to her car and driving away.

Todd stood on the front porch and watched as Jessie drove away from the house. He would give her a few hours to decompress. Surely they, too, would tell her what he had told her. None of this was her fault, and it was asinine for her to think it was.

CHAPTER 44

*H*e'd waited. Todd looked at his watch again, and now it was nearly seven o'clock in the evening and he hadn't heard from Jessie all day.

When he'd watched her pull out of the driveway, he was sure she'd go to her mother, or her sister, and they'd help to mend her wounds. It had to hurt to watch what you'd built go up in flames, but to know that it was because someone was stealing your stuff and their tactics caused the fire, that was a lot to take in. He understood that.

What he didn't understand was her blaming herself for the fire.

Todd picked up the beer he'd been nursing and finished it.

The hours he'd been pacing the house had given him some insight into himself, too.

Jessie was blaming herself for something that wasn't her fault. She was projecting this trauma and taking the blame. The fire was no more her fault than it was his—just like he'd projected his parents' failed relationships on the one he had with Jessie. Their misfortunes weren't his.

He'd taken so much energy, over the years and upon meeting Jessie, pushing people away, because he thought that was what he was supposed to do. He, too, was projecting their problems on his own life and it had cost him relationships in the past. Then he thought of the night Jessie had kicked him out until he worked through it—she just needed to work through this too. But it was killing him.

Todd picked up the bottle and dropped it in the recycle bin as the doorbell chimed.

Jessie would have let herself in, so he didn't want to rush to the door hoping it was her.

Phillip Smythe stood on the other side of the door, civilian clothes on and his ball cap in his hand.

Todd opened the door. "You look like you could use a beer."

A small smile curled up the corner of his mouth. "I most certainly could."

The two men walked back to the kitchen and Todd pulled two beers from the refrigerator. Each man pulled back a chair and sat down.

Phillip twisted the top from his bottle and took a long sip. Todd did the same and then went to work on the label.

"Any news on the *Bridal Mecca*?" Todd asked.

"Not much more than I shared with you earlier. How did Jessie take it?"

Todd shrugged. "You don't see her here, do you?" His response was snarky, and a pang of guilt pierced his stomach. "Sorry. She didn't take it well at all. She thinks it's all her fault."

"She had nothing to do with it."

"It was her studio where the fire started."

"But not by any fault of hers."

Todd took a long pull from his beer. Hadn't he told her that too? Her attitude toward it was wrong—just wrong. How could she even think that way?

"Maybe I should talk to her," Phillip offered.

"And how are you going to change her mind?"

Phillip looked at his beer. "I don't know. Maybe it would just make me feel more useful." He sat back in the chair. "We have nothing to go on. No video of the area. Your cameras melted and the computer in the office was destroyed by the water. They're going through the building to see what's stable and what's not." He scrubbed his hand over his face. "It's like watching someone die."

Todd was glad they had all left. His heart still hurt just thinking of what they'd watched.

"What about Lydia? Is she doing okay?" Todd asked?

Phillip shrugged. "Tyson took her home, and that was the last I'd seen of her. Seriously, this isn't how I wanted to re-introduce myself to her, if you will. I hoped that with her having been gone so long, maybe she'd come back and not hate me so much. In fact, when she opened the door to me, I could have sworn she nearly smiled. But when I told her we needed to get to the *Bridal Mecca* and why, well, that smile never came."

"She'll be okay," Todd assured him. "Now she has something to work on."

"You're right. This is a horrible thing, but it'll keep her busy."

The men finished their beers in silence, and Phillip eventually left. Todd was sure he was only looking for company. Surely his job could be lonely. Perhaps he'd keep that in mind and consider taking him out for a beer every once in a while.

Todd cleaned up the bottles, picked up his keys and his phone, and headed toward his truck. It had been long enough. He needed to find Jessie and find out what was going on. He'd start at her parents' house. Surely that was where she'd gone.

WHEN TODD KNOCKED ON HER PARENTS' door, they seemed surprised to see him standing on the porch alone.

"Why are you looking for Jessie? Where did she go?" her mother asked him and her eyes grew wide with panic.

"She needed some time to think after the fire. I just thought she'd been gone long enough," he tried to assure her in a calm tone, but now he worried as well. "Perhaps she went to Carlie's."

"Let's call her," Carol Hanson said, inviting him in.

They put in the call to Carlie, who hadn't seen her.

Now his chest hurt. After what had happened to Lydia, not knowing Jessie's exact whereabouts began to panic him too.

Her father then walked through the kitchen, his cellphone in hand. "She's with Finn. He just texted me and said she'd been there most of the day. Sounds like they've had a few beers, and he thinks someone should go get her." There was an odd twinkle in his eye when he delivered the news of her whereabouts.

"I'll head over there right now. Where does Finn live?"

~*~

THEY WERE SITTING on Finn's front porch in old wooden rocking chairs when Todd arrived. From the street he could see the redness in her face that was a sign that she'd spent most of the day crying with Finn.

Neither of them stood from their chairs, and he wondered if they could stand. Next to Finn was a bucket of beers on ice, that must have been replenished. Behind them, a box filled with the empties.

It looked like a scene from the front porch of Eric's house when they would all end up there when they were having a bad day. Sometimes the Walker men could talk through their problems. Sometimes they punched each other. The memory humored him.

It bothered him that she had to seek refuge somewhere away from him, but he'd try to understand. She was feeling guilty and everyone else was his family.

But he was there now, ready to take her home.

"Hey, Todd," Finn's voice boomed and slurred.

"Finn."

"She's in good hands," he promised.

Todd nodded as he climbed the steps to the covered porch. "I know she is." He shifted his gaze to Jessie. "Are you about ready to come home now?"

Her lips trembled as she set her beer on the ground. "I just needed some time to think—somewhere other than home."

"I get it. Just next time, tell me where you're going. I was worried."

She nodded and then closed her eyes, no doubt to get her bearings.

Todd walked to her and helped her stand, waiting a moment before he tried to move her. "It looks like you both put a great hurt on that case of beer."

Finn nodded, his eyes only slightly less glazed than Jessie's. "Yeah, we had a good talk. I like you, man. You're good people." Finn raised his beer to Todd in salute.

Without laughing, Todd gave Finn a nod. "I appreciate that." He wrapped his arm around Jessie and started away from the house. "Do you feel okay?"

"I'm fine. Just a little wobbly and a whole lot sad."

"I get that." He opened the door to the truck and helped her in before skirting the front and climbing in the other side. "Are you hungry? Let me know if you're sick so I can pull over."

Leaning her head against the back of the seat, she rolled it to look at him. "I could use a burger."

"I'll get you one."

"And then a long nap."

Now he smiled and let out a chuckle. "I can get you one of those too."

"And I'm sorry."

Todd reached for her hand and gave it a squeeze. "No need to be sorry. You needed to process this."

"I mean, I'm sorry. I just can't marry you."

CHAPTER 45

*T*odd kept his eyes on the road before him. His smile had faded. His heart ached. His chest hurt.

"You do need a nap," he agreed with her through gritted teeth.

"I don't belong in this family. I can't come back from this like they can. I can't do this. I don't belong."

Because he needed to look her in the eye, he pulled over to the side of the road and put the truck in park.

"You need a nap to process this and wear off your drunk."

"I'm not that drunk," she said, and her words slurred again.

"I'm not going to just let you walk out of my life because there was an accident. It's time to rebuild."

Tears were streaming down her cheeks now. "I don't want to rebuild. I don't want to do any of this." She pulled his grandmother's ring from her finger and handed it back to him. "Take me to my sister's house."

"Jessie, just come home."

She shook her head. "No. I don't want to be there with you. I just want to go to Carlie's. You'll get over me," she said and closed her eyes. "This went too fast anyway."

There were no more words. She'd fallen asleep.

He could take her home and put her to bed. When she woke, she'd be none the wiser about what she'd said.

But when he pulled away from the curb, his grandmother's ring on his pinkie, he decided to do as she'd asked.

He called Carlie and warned her they were coming. She was standing on the front step when they pulled up and Todd carried Jessie inside and laid her on the bed in their spare bedroom.

Carlie closed the door and walked with Todd.

"She'll be okay. She's a big woman, but not always emotionally adept when everything goes wrong—because nothing ever goes wrong. But this is how she processed Freddie's death too. It took them two weeks to get her back to school."

He hated that she was hurting, but perhaps that shined a little light on the subject.

"I'll make sure she calls you when she's ready," Carlie promised.

"I'd appreciate that."

"I had a call from Lydia Morgan today," she said before he reached the door. "She sent over emails about another venue for the wedding. *The Garden?*"

Todd chuckled. "It's a beautiful venue."

"I liked the pictures. Pearl also sent over an email that said my dress had been with the seamstress, so it was safe."

"That's good news."

"She'll have the tuxes ready in her temporary location for the attendants, and new bridesmaid's dresses as well."

"It seems as if my sister and Lydia went right to work."

"They have a lot of pending things to put into place."

Todd leaned in and kissed Carlie on the cheek. "She thinks this is her fault, and it's not. It's only a roadblock for my sisters and the rest of them. Tell her they're moving forward. Make her move forward, even if she doesn't want to move on with me."

Carlie narrowed her eyes. "She said that?"

He held up his finger to show her his grandmother's ring. "She said that."

"Give her a couple of days. You're too good a catch to let go."

~*~

AND TODD GAVE it a couple days. He lived in her house, surrounded by her things, but she wasn't around. The first day, he didn't text her or call her. By the second and third day, he'd only sent her one text a day. *I love you*, which had gone unanswered.

Every morning, he'd met Lydia at the office her mother kept in a building she owned. It always amazed Todd that between Lydia and her mother, they owned half of the town.

They went over the many events that Todd had contracted over the past year and sorted them out so they could find accommodations for them. Most people were understanding of what had happened and were amazed that they had been contacted and considered. But there were a few that, upon hearing of the fire, had run out and made other arrangements.

Todd found a new home for the church that had been using the hall on Sundays, and the few social groups that used it during the week.

The work kept his mind off losing Jessie and watching Lydia step right in and do what she did best lifted his heart.

Pearl walked through the office door, two large coffee cups in hand. She handed one to Lydia, and the other to him.

"She doesn't miss a step, does she?" Pearl nodded toward Lydia with a smile.

"I've never met anyone so organized."

Pearl pursed her lips and narrowed her eyes.

Todd laughed. "Except for you. You are the queen of it."

The smile returned. "Thank you. Have you talked to Jessie?"

"She won't talk to me. I suppose this weekend I'll move back out by the ranch, and she can at least move home. I have someone wanting to lease my place. I guess I'll have to let that go. I thought she'd come around, but she still thinks she's to blame for everything. I wish she could see you all working."

His sister and Lydia exchanged looks, and he wondered what they had planned for him. But they said nothing else.

Pearl sat with them for the next hour as they went over wedding venues, brides' wishes, dresses that were on reorder or hadn't been on site.

Then, at one o'clock, they both turned to him. "You are in charge, cowboy," Lydia gave him a stern patting on the back.

"Where are you going?"

"We have a meeting. There is a list on the desk of calls to make and orders to put in. I'll see you in the morning."

And with that, Pearl and Lydia hurried out of the office leaving him alone, abruptly.

Todd shook his head. He would never understand women.

CHAPTER 46

*J*essie's heart raced in her chest as she looked at the message on her cellphone and confirmed that she was in the right place.

Pearl had texted her that there was an insurance meeting for all tenants of the *Bridal Mecca* and that it was mandatory.

Jessie had been at her sister's all week, and when she'd announced that she was leaving for a meeting, her sister had all but pushed her out the door.

She'd never been one to recover quickly from something traumatic, but she thought her sister could have given her a few more days before she'd gotten sassy with her.

Then again, she'd been moping around the house and her sister was busy working and trying to finalize wedding plans. Lydia and Pearl had stepped right up and made sure that Carlie's wedding would go off without a hitch. They'd even gone as far as having change of venue cards printed so they could mail them out to their guests in plenty of time.

Perhaps Jessie was simply mad that she didn't have her camera so she couldn't even take pictures of her sister's wedding —well not if she didn't stop moping and went and bought one.

Jessie climbed from her car and walked toward the building they had given her the address to. A smile formed on her lips when she saw the sign on the door, *Pearl's Bridal Boutique.*

It hadn't even been a full week since they'd all lost everything, and here Pearl had a storefront.

When she opened the door, she was amazed that the entire store was filled with dresses. It was set up much like the other store, with a makeshift back area for try-ons and fittings.

"We're back here," Pearl called.

Jessie sucked in a long, deep breath before walking toward the back of the store. Everyone was there, including her mother and sister. Certainly they weren't involved in the insurance meeting.

"I thought we were discussing insurance."

Lydia waved her hand through the air as if to ward off the thought. "Insurance will take forever to get to us. The longer you're in business, the more you learn. Ellie is on that. She's already filing what she needs on behalf of my company to get the building rebuilt."

Jessie nodded. She'd been in touch with her agent, and he too had said it would move as quickly as possible, but she hadn't believed his tone.

"So then what are we meeting about?" Jessie asked as all eyes were on her, and each woman wore a strange little smile.

Pearl opened the door to the little room she was using for a fitting room, but Jessie had to assume it might have been a closet.

Hanging on the hook was the wedding dress Jessie had picked.

"We had to reorder the dress, but you need to try it on," Pearl said.

Jessie felt the blood drain from her face. "I—I don't think that's a good idea."

Pearl moved toward her, handing her a glass of champagne from the tray on the table. "Why?"

"I'm not getting married."

No one in the room seemed surprised by her admission of that. So why had they presented her with the dress?

"He tells us you think the fire is all your fault."

"It started in my shop."

"After someone kicked open your back door, took your computer and caused your lamp to fall over. You weren't there for that." Pearl's voice was matter-of-fact, but didn't have an unkind tone. "They caught the son-of-a-bitch too," she added. "One more reason for champagne."

Jessie could feel the sting of tears. "You all lost everything. Everything you've worked years and years for. You let me into your circle and your building, and now it's all gone."

Pearl shook her head. "Look around. The circle is still here."

Jessie looked around the room, and sympathetic eyes looked up at her.

"Aren't you all mad?"

Lydia moved in to stand next to Pearl. "Inconvenienced for a bit. This can't take us down. I've been through worse."

That made Jessie's chest ache. "I didn't mean to be insensitive."

"You're not. You've been through worse too. I remember your brother. He was a nice kid. Your mom told us how long it took you to come around then, too. And I know since Big Finn had his heart attack, you've been taking care of him."

Jessie bit down on her lip. "I was afraid I'd lose him, too."

Pearl reached for her hand. "We're all going to rebuild. It's part of life. And take all the time you need to heal, but not at the cost of your friends, family, and especially Todd."

"He doesn't need someone who can't handle things."

"You're handling it the way you need to," Pearl said, smiling at her. "But he loves you, and he will be right by your side to help you through it."

She missed him. She loved him so much she'd wondered if she hurt more because her studio was gone or because she'd pushed Todd away.

"Jessie," her mother's voice drew her attention. "We have something for you."

She held up a box with a bright red bow and handed it to her.

Jessie took it, her vision now blurred by tears. As she lifted the lid off, she saw the familiar comfort of her camera.

"I went to the man who sold you the last one. He had all the records of what you'd bought," her mother said with eyes filled with tears. "Don't give up."

Jessie set the box on the table and went to her mother and sister and enveloped them both in a hug.

Her mother eased back. "And now you'll take the money we offered you and start over. You have a house and you and Todd will be very comfortable there until insurance comes in and can repay your investment."

Before she could even speak, Pearl had taken her hand. "C'mon, I want to show you something."

She pulled Jessie toward the front door and outside. They walked to the next retail space in the building where Pearl's store had relocated, and Pearl took out a key and opened the door.

They stepped inside and Jessie looked around the empty space that must have been vacant for a while by the amount of dust.

"What is this?"

Pearl wrapped an arm around her. "Your new studio. I know the landlord, and she'll cut you a good deal."

Jessie turned to her. "Lydia owns this?"

Pearl laughed and shook her head. "No. This one is mine. And I'd be honored if my sister-in-law was right next door to me."

"Pearl…"

"You can't say no. You can take some time to think about it, but you can't say no."

"And I would like it if you'd still be her sister-in-law," Todd's voice came from the door.

Jessie turned to see him standing there surrounded by the

other women, and at that moment the tears flooded back and rolled down her cheeks.

She'd missed him so much, and she hadn't realized just how much until she saw his face.

Todd moved to her. "I love you. I realize you had to process this, but see, no one blames you."

Jessie wiped her cheek with the tips of her fingers. "This is all so much."

"This is what's it's like to be part of a big, crazy family," he said with a laugh. "I'm not the only one who loves you."

"You still love me?"

"God, nothing could make me not love you."

"I've been horrible."

"You've been hurting," he confirmed as he rested his hands on her hips and her arms came to his neck. "And now you're healing."

Jessie let out a breath and rested her forehead to his. "I do love you."

"Good," he said as he stepped back and dropped to one knee in front of her. "Then, will you agree to marry me—again?"

He held out the ring she'd given him back the day she said she didn't want to marry him.

Covering her mouth with her hand she looked down at the man, surrounded by the women who loved him. If she married him she inherited all of them, and that was only a bonus, she thought. If it were just him, she'd want him just as much.

"Yes. Yes, I will marry you."

He slid the ring back on her finger and stood, picking her up and swinging her around in circles.

The women around them cheered and applauded before enveloping them both in hugs.

She'd been crazy for telling him she didn't want to marry him. There had been nothing she wanted more than to be his wife.

*J*essie wasn't sure how it had been possible, but business had been even busier after the fire. Perhaps people just wanted to see if they were still the same unit they had been when all of their businesses were housed in the same building.

Lydia and her mother had bought one more reception venue, and when the *Bridal Mecca* was fully operational again, it would be another source of income.

Todd pushed open the door to her studio and stepped inside. He was dressed in a suit, and she couldn't have imagined he could be sexier than usual—but he was.

"Do you have everything?" he asked.

Jessie checked her bags one more time. "I think I do." She zipped up her camera bag and handed it to him.

"You look beautiful," he said taking in the sight of her in her bridesmaid dress.

"This is going to inhibit me more than help me," she said brushing her hands over her skirt.

"Remember, you and your sister are both getting what you want. You're not having to stand up on the altar and you get to take the pictures, and she still has her sister in her wedding. It's a win, win."

Jessie pressed her hand to her fluttering stomach. "Why am I so nervous?"

"This is your sister that's getting married. It's a big thing."

"You're right. It is a big thing."

They carried her equipment out to his truck, and then Jessie closed and locked the door. "Did I tell you that Missy wants me to take pictures while she's having her baby?" Jessie asked as she carefully climbed into his truck, careful not to bunch up her dress.

Todd looked at her with a bemused expression. "Would you want to do that?"

She shrugged. "It would be a first."

"That's weird to me."

"You're a guy."

"That I am." He started the engine and put the truck into drive. Pulling away from the curb, he took her hand in his. "I have something I want to show you on the way to the church."

"Do we have time?"

"Yeah. It's on the way."

He drove away from the center of town and down a few residential streets, and came to park in front of a two-story house with a two-car, attached garage.

The green, lush yard made a perfect welcoming mat. The bright, burnt orange door, and the flower boxes that bloomed under the windows accentuated the gray siding.

"What is this?" she asked turning to see him smiling at her.

"It goes on the market tomorrow," he said. "It's in our price range, sort of." He chuckled. "There's enough room to start a family there and we wouldn't outgrow it right away."

"It's situated near my parents, my sister, and Finn," she offered matter-of-factly and Todd nodded.

"That it is." He lifted her hand to his lips and pressed a kiss to her fingers. "Would you be interested in seeing it tomorrow?"

She looked back at the house and imagined standing in that doorway welcoming visitors, or watching her children play in the front yard.

"I would."

Todd shifted his glance toward the house and then back at her. "I have to admit, I assumed I'd be the only Walker that never found true love. And I get that Eric was in his forties before he did, but I'd just come to grips with it. But the moment your sister brought you to the *Bridal Mecca* I knew something big would happen in my life."

"You're a smooth talker, Mr. Walker."

"I mean every word."

"Let's go watch my sister get married, dance all night at the reception, and toast to new beginnings."

"That sounds like a perfect day."

She looked back at the house. "And then let's come back tomorrow and take some measurements."

Todd laughed. "Why measurements?"

"Look how big that front window is. I need to know what size Christmas tree to buy. It's going to be ostentatious."

"I love you, Jessie. I can't wait to live there with you."

"And I love you. Thanks for being stubborn enough to hang on to me." She leaned in and kissed him. "Now, let's get going. I want to see how lovely my sister looks in her dress."

We hope you enjoyed Masterpiece.
Here is a sneak peak at the final book in the
Walker Family Series,
At Last.

AT LAST

*I*t had been hard enough to stand in that very spot and watch everything she and her friends had built burn to the ground. But nearly two months after the fire, Lydia Morgan thought it was even more heart-breaking to watch progress—which meant the existing structure had to come down.

Ella Walker, her lawyer, had been key in making sure that the insurance company was working on Lydia's behalf, and that of the others who lost their business that early morning in May.

She'd been on site every day since that fire. It certainly hadn't been the way she'd wanted to reengage herself with the community after having been gone for nearly a year, but it wasn't something she could control. And part of her therapy was learning how to let go of control and adjust.

Lydia owned most of the town, both the buildings and the businesses. She had taken after her mother in that sense, together their names were on quite a bit of real estate.

The *Bridal Mecca* had been a special project she had taken on with Pearl Walker. It had been a big deal for a Morgan and a Walker to go into business together. The families had feuded for years. It had not only been one of the most profitable partnerships Lydia had ever entered into, but it also grew her family, literally. Pearl had fallen in love with Lydia's brother Tyson, who was also one of the owners of the building.

Now it was nothing but a pile of rubble that would absolutely be rebuilt.

Lydia walked back to her car, pulling off the hard hat she kept in her car. She ran her fingers through her short crop of hair, which Audrey had cut just the day before. Lydia always wore her hair short, but while she'd been gone, she'd given up that control too, and had let it grow. After two months, it had been time to take back that part of her identity.

Just as she opened the door to her car, the familiar personal truck of Phillip Smythe pulled into the lot.

A year ago, she would have climbed into her car and driven over the curb to escape talking to him. But that was then. Her therapy had carried her through that as well—her misguided relationship with the man.

Phillip stepped out of his truck. His police uniform replaced with a pair of jeans and a pearl-snapped shirt. The buckle on his belt was reminiscent of the days he'd team roped and won. His boots were worn, and the bill of his ball cap shielded his eyes.

His long legs carried him toward her, slowly, as if he were still afraid to talk to her.

She wasn't sure if his apprehension was because he was never sure if she'd bite his head off, or if he was still spooked by what had happened to her a year ago.

Again, part of her therapy covered her feelings for Phillip Smythe, and she had plenty of them.

"Looks like they're making progress," he said, lifting the bill of his cap to reveal those gray eyes she remembered from long ago.

"I suppose. It's hard to think progress means taking down what was there."

Phillip tucked his hands into the front pockets of his jeans and rocked back on his heels. "Your hair looks good."

"Thanks. I needed to return to some normality. I have no idea how other women wear their hair long."

"Short has always suited you," he complimented, and she watched as he ground his heel into the dirt. "Are you headed out?"

"I have a meeting with a new bride looking for a venue, but that's not until this afternoon."

"And you have a few to choose from."

She smiled wide. "You know, my goal is to own the entire town."

"You're well on your way."

"I'll see you around," she said as she pulled open the door to her car and climbed in.

Phillip walked toward the fence that had been put up around the shell of the *Bridal Mecca* and Lydia sat in her car and let out a long breath. It had been nearly fifteen years since she'd had a civil conversation with the man, and she'd allowed herself to be comforted by his arm around her the night that the *Bridal Mecca* burnt down. She figured he'd come around more often after that. He'd been everywhere she'd turned for more than a decade, but the past two months his presence had been sparse.

It was as foreign to have him stay away from her as it was for her to want him around—at least a little bit.

After she'd been kidnapped, sexually assaulted, and left for dead, she realized holding a grudge against Phillip was a waste of her time and energy. Any anger and resentment she had toward him had always been her fault.

The therapy she'd gone through had taught her how to approach their past, and to accept that he was a daily part of her life.

She supposed if she wanted to spend time with him, and truly see if her therapy had worked, she would need to lead the conversation.

Re-opening her car door, Lydia stepped out and stood in

front of her car. "Hey, Smythe," she yelled to be heard over the construction noise.

He turned to look at her, and then walked toward her.

"You're not on duty, huh?"

Phillip shook his head. "No. I took a personal day. I have something going on this evening."

"Well then you have some time."

"Time for what?"

"Why don't you have lunch with me? I'd love some company, and I want to try that new Greek place on the edge of town."

Phillip thoughtfully bit down on his lip. "I could go for that. I can just meet you over there."

She'd have offered to drive, but maybe meeting him would be best. What if she found being in his presence for more than a few minutes at a time made her hate him again. What if seeing her broken had pushed him away for good?

"I'll meet you there," she agreed and watched as he walked to his truck.

She knew he'd never drive away until she had, so she pulled out of the parking lot and started driving toward the restaurant. Phillip followed her in his truck, and when she'd look back in her mirror her stomach tightened.

It had been a long year of healing. She couldn't go back on her fifteen years of anger and just expect that he'd accept that she wanted to be friends. There were also secrets she still kept, and things would certainly change between them if he found out about them.

Lydia gripped her steering wheel tighter. This was lunch. Lunch with a man she'd pushed away for years. She had learned she had to take things one moment at a time. This was just one moment in the rest of her life.

Lunch.

She could handle lunch.

ABOUT THE AUTHOR

Bestselling Author Bernadette Marie is known for building families readers want to be part of. Her series The Keller Family has graced bestseller charts since its release in 2011. Since then she has authored and published over thirty-five books. The married mother of five sons promises romances with a Happily Ever After always...and says she can write it because she lives it.

Obsessed with the art of writing and the business of publishing, chronic entrepreneur Bernadette Marie established her own publishing house, 5 Prince Publishing, in 2011 to bring her own work to market as well as offer an opportunity for fresh voices in fiction to find a home as well. Bernadette Marie is also the owner of Illumination Author Events which offers industry education as well as smaller intimate author/reader events.

When not immersed in the writing/publishing world, Bernadette Marie and her husband are shuffling their five hockey playing boys around town to practices and games as well as running their family business of carwash locations. She is a lover of a good stout craft beer and might be slightly addicted to chocolate.